Dreams of the Sleepless

Elmer Seward

Bay Rivers Publishing

ISBN: 9780692243923

Cover art was created utilizing Canva AI Image Generator.

In the twilight between the heart's dark secrets and reality's harsh light, lie the dreams of the sleepless.

Now

I punctuate the sentence, period at the end. I lift the pen and look up. Outside in the parking lot, the car at the pumps. Did I see it at our last stop? Black Ford. How many black Fords are there in the world? Millions. I watch a moment longer. Nothing unusual. Looking down, I reread my last sentence and then continue, *Sometimes, I'm better now. Really, I am.* I want to write, *Sometimes, I see monsters at night*, but I leave it unsaid. I choose the glass half-full. He would like that. I sign the card using some other man's name, not my own. A glance at the parking lot. The black Ford is gone. The muscles in my neck uncoil as I release one long breath. Looking down again, I flip the card over and study the sepia image. It's a reprint of a vintage postcard depicting International Bridge in Fort Kent Maine, the end of U.S. Highway 1. The symmetry of it all makes me smile. I slip the card in the mail slot and marvel at how different life is now. Now? Now, my life is measured in postcards with quickly jotted lines. Then? Well, *then…* there wasn't much to measure.

Then

Hot Coffee, Black

The bright light spilled from the diner's windows into the dark street, a beacon calling to storm-tossed travelers in the night. Calling to life's broken souls. Calling to me. It was early, and the small restaurant was almost empty. Like most diners, it was unremarkable. There were rows of booths along the windows to the left and a counter with upholstered bar stools to the right. The once red upholstery, more like a dry riverbed, cracked and a muddy rust color, revealed years of wear. Beyond the counter a large serving window opened into the kitchen. The counter wrapped around at the far end and met the windows just beyond the booths.

I pushed through the door to brewing coffee's friendly greeting. Country music played softly in the background. I couldn't quite place the song. I was sure that I'd heard its sad lyrics and melody before, but details like that were lost on me now. Beyond the order window, I heard a woman's voice singing perfect, quiet harmony.

A solitary customer sat hunched over his cup near the far end of the counter, a rumpled newspaper lying abandoned next to him. He was tall and wiry. His short-cropped, white hair and beard stood in stark contrast to his dark brown skin. His dingy white shirt hung loosely from his frail frame.

He'd probably been a much bigger man when he bought that shirt years ago but was now a shadow of his younger self. He turned toward me as I stood just inside the doorway. His face like a fallow field was deeply furrowed. Slowly he studied me in the way that he might study the obituaries, his friends long since passed on. Nothing interesting, just grateful not to see a younger photo of himself smiling back from the pages. Expressionless, he turned back to his coffee. Most people coming to a diner, even at this early hour, are in a rush to eat and get on with the day. His slow, deliberate manner told me that he was in no hurry to go anywhere. Maybe, like me, he had nowhere to go.

I slid into the first booth as far from the old man as I could. I wanted to be alone. Although he seemed more interested in the depths of the dark liquid that sat before him, I decided to be cautious. Sometimes people in small towns can be chatty. They like to pry. I picked up the laminated menu, sticky with yesterday's syrup, and scanned it. The door behind me creaked open. A guy in khakis and a black polo shirt walked past and took a seat several booths away, facing me. I could feel his eyes on me. Not wanting to make eye contact, I looked out into the deep blackness through the window. The sun would be up soon, but, for now, the nighttime backdrop and lighted windowpane formed a dark, shadowy looking glass. I could see his faint reflection. He held a menu but was clearly looking above it in my direction. It was the kind of scrutiny I anticipated as a stranger in a small town. The suspicious glances, the whispered disapproval, the blatant glares—I knew them well.

I glanced down at the predictable menu—eggs, bacon, sausage, and pancakes. The prices seemed fair, but no price is a good price when you're broke. My hands began trembling. Laying the menu on the table, I placed them on either side, applying pressure to try to calm them with little success. Worthless hands! I needed to see how much money I had, but my hands were useless. I laid my messenger bag on the table. The once lighter gray nylon was now dark and stained from long hours on the road. The material frayed in fuzzy tufts around the edges and my random jumble of possessions peered out through small holes that formed near the gaping seams. Fighting the tremors, Trying to sort through the odd collection of items and fish out what little money I had left was useless. My hands wouldn't cooperate. I dumped the side pocket of the bag on the table. The contents clattered out, some scattering onto the floor. I glanced up. The old man and polo-shirt guy were both glaring at me.

The door behind me banged open and a booming voice announced, "Babe, your lover boy is back!" The booming voice swaggered past me wearing a brown deputy's uniform. He was a large man. Probably played football in an earlier life, but his current heft wouldn't qualify as football worthy. Too many years of sitting in a cruiser. He strode past me, polo shirt, and the old guy as if we weren't even there. I caught

4

the distinct aroma of alcohol as he passed. He glanced around without seeing the three of us. "Where are you, babe?" He plopped down on one of the stools at the end of the counter. The edges of the seat disappeared under his cruiser-trained rump. He boomed again, "What does a fella have to do to get service around here?"

An attractive woman, late twenties, maybe early thirties strode out of the kitchen area. She was tall and shapely but not cartoonishly so. She wouldn't be one of the scantily clad women in popular beer commercials. Nor would you find her adorning the pages of swimsuit calendars. But her gently curving figure was attractive. With hands on hips, she glared at the deputy. Then in surprise, she looked beyond to where I sat and then over at polo shirt. "Oh, I'm so sorry. I didn't hear ya'll come in. I'll be with you in just a sec,"

I rushed to pick up the things I'd dumped from my bag. My hands worked as well as mittens picking up toothpicks. I struggled to put everything back in the bag. Reaching items strewn on the floor was even more challenging. I left the money on the table – two ones and some loose change.

As the waitress slipped from behind the counter and headed toward me, the deputy shouted, "Hey, how about me?"

She made no reply but approached with a weary smile, more show than substance. This was probably a smile practiced day after day for perhaps years on end, asking the same tired questions only to hear the same tired responses. This diner seemed frozen in time, a place where each day was like the one before, and she was the silent witness to the mundane comings and goings in other people's lives.

As she slid up to the table, she was apologetic. "I'm so sorry. What can I get you this mornin'?"

I placed my trembling hands under the table, grasping my knees, so she wouldn't notice. Pretending to study the menu, I said, "I'll just have coffee, black."

"OK, hun, I'll be right back with your coffee." I exhaled in relief as she moved off to take polo shirts' order. Placing my hands on the table, I applied downward pressure, willing them to be still. Moments later, she drew a cup from the large brewing pot near the end of the counter and brought it to my table. By the time the coffee arrived, the tremors were mostly gone. Raising the cup with both hands to steady it, I sipped the steaming coffee slowly.

The waitress found her way behind the counter, busying herself loading napkin holders and preparing silverware.

The deputy called out, "Come on, babe. Is this any way to treat the man you love?"

The waitress continued with her back to him.

He stood. "How about my order?"

The waitress turned slowly, her head cocked to one side, a dead expression on her face. "OK, Jeb, what do you want?"

Babe, I want YOU," he cackled. This was all some funny game for him.

The waitress shot back with a flat voice that matched her expression, "I'm not on the menu." She turned back to her work.

Something snapped in the deputy. Where there was once sadistic laughter, there was now rage. "Don't turn your back on me," he threatened. In the next few empty seconds, you could feel a violent eruption building. It was like watching the frenzied spikes of a seismometer just moments before a sleeping volcano explodes. "I said, don't turn your back on me!" He reached across the counter grabbing her with his left hand and spinning her around so violently that she fell into a stack of dishes, sending them crashing onto the floor.

She screamed. "Jeb, let go! You're going to break my arm! Jeb, stop!"

The more she wailed, the harder he wrenched her arm. She buckled and twisted trying to free herself. All the while, she uselessly flailed at him with her free hand. Each time she swung, he would apply more painful pressure. Sobbing and screaming, she thrashed uselessly to free herself.

The old guy at the counter yelled, "Jeb, leave her alone."

Jeb shot back, "Shut up, old man!" never turning from his tormenting.

I gulped down the last of my coffee. This was a good time for me to leave. I didn't know these people and didn't want to know them. This was their problem, not mine. Leaving the two bills on the table, I shoveled the loose change into my bag. She deserved a tip after a morning like this. I stood and hurried toward the door while the chorus of wails accompanied by shouted curses from her tormentor rose. My hand was on the door when it happened. I hated it but couldn't stop it. I'd been an empty man for months, dead inside. But now, with my hand on the door, I felt a growing anger. Every emotion that I'd buried deep within me came rushing out in a torrent. Spinning around, I rushed toward the deputy. My brain screamed, *NO, NO, NO, don't do this! He's got a gun! You're going to get yourself killed!* But at that moment, there really wasn't much left of my life. I literally had nothing to lose.

The deputy, his back toward me, was completely engrossed in his torture. He leaned across the counter. His left hand shackled the waitress in its grip. His right hand on the counter supported his upper body. I guessed he had me by about fifty pounds, but most of that wasn't muscle. As I reached him, I grabbed his right hand with mine and pulled it out from under him twisting up behind his back. At the same time, I grabbed his hair with my left hand, shoving his head downward toward the counter as he fell forward. My adrenaline must have spiked because his head hit the counter with a sickening thud. Dazed, he went limp, releasing the waitress and slumping onto the counter. I had to move fast. I unsnapped his holster and removed his gun. The waitress stood frozen, mouth open and eyes wide, a look of horror. My eyes darted around the restaurant. The large coffee pot stood next to me. I removed the lid and dropped the pistol into the hot coffee, splashing the steaming brew all over the counter. The deputy slumped to the floor, as I released him. Removing his handcuffs from his belt, I cuffed his right hand to the foot of one of the stools. Panic struck me as he moaned. I struggled to remove his key ring from his belt. The tremors had returned, and I fumbled to free the ring. His eyes opened briefly as his hand clawed at my arm. Then he went limp as his eyes rolled upward. Jerking and twisting, I finally came away with the collection of keys. I was banking on the handcuff and the cruiser keys being on the ring. Exhaling with relief, I stood and dropped them into the steaming coffee pot.

I looked up at the waitress and said, "You might not want to serve this. Could be a bit strong." She stood frozen, mouth open and eyes as big as the full moon hung just above the summer horizon. The deputy moaned again and began to stir. It was time for me to vanish.

I turned and walked toward the door. The old guy had swiveled on his seat to face me, his weary expression gone. There was a glimmer in his eyes, and a wry smile crept across his face. I glanced down at the floor to avoid eye contact but noticed that as I strode past that he turned on his stool to watch me leave.

ELMER SEWARD

    I stepped out into the heavy, humid air. There was a faint sliver of orange along the jagged horizon. It would be daylight soon. I needed to melt into the night before there was no darkness left. The tremors were back, and I shivered despite the warmth of the night air. The flutter of a bird, the snapping of a twig — I jumped at every sound, glancing back for my pursuer.

Dreams' Graveyard

The sun had been up for hours, and the summer heat was rising. I sat in my small, bare cabin, waiting. Waiting for the deputy to arrive and kill me. But the hours passed and there was no deputy. He hadn't really seen me. Maybe he didn't know who blindsided him. Maybe he had one or two enemies and suspected them. Maybe I was fooling myself. I was a stranger in a small town. I'd be suspected of everything. But if I wound up dead, wouldn't it point back to him? After all, there were three witnesses to our earlier confrontation. That might be my saving grace, but I wasn't betting on it. A stranger in this town could vanish and nobody would ever know… or even care. I'd stay as far from him as I could.

I looked around my tiny rental. I guess you could say it had a Great Room. The bed, a sink, a rickety table and two wooden chairs, an old stove, and a refrigerator – all in one room. There were three small windows, one on each end of the cabin and one on the back wall opposite the door. One of the end windows gave little outside light because an old air conditioning unit took up most of the space. The unit was too big to fit neatly in the window, so someone had cut a piece of Plexiglas to fill the space above it. Over the years, the Plexiglas had clouded and was no longer transparent. The unit hummed and clattered when it ran, but it worked, and I was thankful for it. At least the cabin did have a separate, small bathroom in a back corner. There was a small shower stall, toilet and sink with a metal medicine cabinet hung above it. The place was sparse, but it was all that I could afford. The rent had taken most of my money, and I was days away from my next benefits payment. How could I have been so stupid. I'd lost track of time… again. And I'd spent most of my money before more would come in… again.

I was desperate. Picking up my messenger bag, I dumped the contents onto the table. I sorted through the pile of mostly worthless items and separated the money. After my big spending cup of coffee for two dollars, I only had seventy-six cents left. That would have to feed me for nearly two weeks. Or was it three weeks? I sat for a moment, elbows on the table and my head in my hands. There was only one thing to do. I'd head into town. I really didn't want to run into the deputy, but daylight with others around would be safer than nighttime alone.

As I stepped out of the cabin I nodded to my next-door neighbors. Best neighbors I'd ever had, quiet and undemanding. They knew how to keep a secret. They were dead. A small family cemetery that was slowly being consumed by the surrounding underbrush lay just beyond the dirt clearing in front of the cabin. There were a few very small stone markers, but most were wooden and badly decomposed. Time and weather had obliterated the names and dates. The most recent marker was inscribed

MARTHA GROVER
1962-2001
"I AM THE RESURRECTION AND THE LIFE."

Ironic, I thought. She seemed dead to me.

The dirt lane that led to the main road was dusty and hot. It was clear that it hadn't rained here in a while. I kicked up little clouds of fine dirt as I shuffled down the winding lane. It ran through a dense pine forest with thick underbrush. Small white and yellow blossoms of wild honeysuckle speckled the dense foliage on both sides. Their fragrance lay heavy on the humid air. Fine dust filled the grooves of tire ruts from earlier residents' cars. Weeds and vines obliterated the path in places. It was obvious that no one had lived in this cabin for a while. It was strange how this place could be so isolated and yet be so close to town.

I stepped out of the lane onto the paved highway. There was more of a break in the trees and the sun beat down on me. It was hot with heavy, clinging humidity that left me wet with perspiration. I walked alone. The highway was all mine. It was a stretch of worn, faded asphalt with deep, overgrown ditches running along the narrow shoulders. No cars going either direction. This had probably been a busy highway at one time but after the interstate was completed just a few miles away, traffic dwindled to mostly locals. Not far up the highway, I hit the outskirts of town. There were a few scattered houses, mostly small and in need of attention. Their bare, weathered wood looked like it had never seen a coat of paint. Windows without curtains. Yards with waist-high weeds. You'd have thought they were deserted, except for the telltale signs of laundry hanging from clotheslines in the back or a car parked on the gravel drives. I pressed on toward what was once the business district. The houses here were larger and better maintained. As I passed a long picket fence with peeling paint and missing pickets, a deep voice called out, "Hello, neighbor." It had been a quiet walk, and the sudden, disembodied voice startled me. My alarm must have been noticeable because before I could turn to find the speaker, he called out, "Sorry, didn't mean to spook you."

I glanced over to where the voice originated. It was the old guy from the diner. He reclined in a rocking chair on the porch of a two-story home that sat not far from the road. It looked like it had been a very nice home at one time, big and stately. It was not a plantation house by any stretch of the imagination but was built in plantation style. The porch ran the entire length of the house with tall columns that supported an impressive overhang. Like other houses along the way, this house had seen better days. The white paint was peeling and the shutters, the ones that were still in place, had faded from black to a chalky gray. Occasional bricks were missing from the walkway and the steps leading up to the porch.

I didn't want to socialize, so I nodded and said, "Morning," as I turned to continue toward town.

He called out again, "That was really something at Duke's this morning."

I turned and gave him a puzzled look.

Seeing my confusion he added, "You know, the diner… Duke's." He had that same twinkle in his eyes and wry smile on his face that I'd seen earlier. He was getting some strange pleasure out of all this. I hadn't even paid attention to the name of the diner. For months now details were lost on me, just not important.

Not wanting a conversation, I just said, "Yep, it sure was."

I began to turn but halted as he started up again. "You be careful, son. Jeb has a mean streak and doesn't like being made the fool." His expression had changed from amused to serious. The old man wasn't telling me anything I hadn't already realized.

I thanked him for the advice and turned again. This time he let me go, and I walked on past a few more houses, crossing the street just past Duke's.

Bethany Crossing was like so many rural Virginia towns. It had once been a busy, if small, farming town. When tobacco was at its height, farming had been profitable and the few stores in town prospered. Over the years, the rise of large business-owned farming operations, the decline in the demand for tobacco, competition from foreign imports, and the migration of jobs to bigger cities like Richmond and Norfolk had eroded the beleaguered town like torrential rains slurrying rich topsoil from the fields.

The little town consisted of ten to fifteen storefronts running down the main street. Many of them were now abandoned. Once brightly decorated display windows now sat empty and dark. There were others with raggedly boarded windows revealing shards of broken glass. I stood for a moment thinking how the town was so much like me, half dead and clinging on to what little life was left.

One store seemed to have survived by diversifying, Willard's Feed and Supply. It had signs in the window indicating that it was part fishing and hunting equipment, part feed and farming supplies, and the part that I had come for. There were two small neon signs in the window. One flashed, WE BUY GOLD, and the other simply read, PAWN. As I stepped through the door into the dark, empty store, a balding, heavy-set man looked up from his newspaper and glared at me above the rim of his glasses.

After a couple of uncomfortable seconds, he said, "Can I help you?" I suspected this was Willard and he knew every person within a fifty-mile radius. However, he didn't know me, and I think that threw him for a moment.

I motioned toward the sign in the window. "It says this is a pawn shop." It was more of a question than a statement.

"Yep," he answered, and there was another awkward pause.

"I'd like to pawn this watch." I slipped my Seiko Chronograph from my wrist and handed it to Willard who had ambled over to the counter in front of me. He looked at the black face of the watch and then studied the stainless-steel band and the reverse side. It wasn't a high-end watch like a Tag Heur, but it cost over two hundred dollars new. It was one of very few remnants of a more stable, happier time in my life. I figured I could get at least a hundred for it.

After looking the watch over several times, Willard spoke up. "Nice watch. So, you want to pawn it?"

"Yeah, I just need a loan."

Willard continued to study the watch. "How much you want for it?"

"I was thinking a hundred."

He looked at me over the rim of his glasses again and chuckled. "It might be worth a hundred, but folks around here don't have that kind of money to spend on a watch. If you don't repay the loan, I'll lose money 'cause I'll never sell it for that. I'll give you twenty-five."

"Twenty-five? You're kidding, right?"

Willard responded with a silent stare. My heart sank. I was counting on the watch getting me through until my next benefits payment came in. Twenty-five dollars wasn't going to come close to what I needed. I'd take what I could get, but I haggled with him for several minutes, trying to work the loan up a bit. I managed to talk him up to thirty-five dollars.

As he drew up the paperwork, I closed my eyes and could clearly see the day I got the watch.

* *. *

It had been a surprise gift for my birthday. I'd secretly longed for it. Every time we went to the mall, I'd study it through the jewelry store window, trying hard not to let her notice. I'd wait for her to become entranced by the sparkling rings and necklaces and then pretend to pass the time browsing while she fantasized about dancing in fancy gowns and glittering jewels. I never told her how much I wanted the watch. No need to. We didn't have the money. But somehow, she knew. Secretly, she saved for months, setting a little aside each payday from the grocery money. She knew that I hated peanut butter, so she kept the savings in a Ziploc bag inside an empty peanut butter jar in the pantry. For months, it sat there, and I never knew. The morning of my birthday, she was like a child in a candy store, giddy and excited. You would have thought that it was her birthday. Her eyes sparkled as she handed me the narrow, slender box with the simple silver bow. She bit her lower lip in anticipation, and as I slid the bow down the box, she quietly said, "I love you sooooo much. Happy birthday, baby." I opened the box and then looked up in amazement. She was beaming, so excited about the triumph of her surprise. More than a watch, it was a gift of love. That was the gift she always gave, even later when I became a brooding, unwilling recipient.

* *. *

I sighed at this recollection. Sadly, it hadn't been that long ago measured in years, but measured in suffering, it was another life away.

I looked down at the second-hand items displayed in the long glass counter and on the wall behind it. One item in the case caught my eye, a sparkling engagement ring. Perhaps it had once promised a happy future but was now a cast-off reminder of broken promises. Or maybe it was a treasured symbol of eternal love, tearfully surrendered by a young widow desperate to feed her children. It sat in the case with other rings, necklaces, and bracelets – some discarded because they were no longer wanted. Others treasured but sold to keep body and soul together. Here in this dark, cold setting, was the graveyard of people's dreams, loves, and lives.

As I stepped into the sunlight, I was thirty-five dollars richer and yet much poorer. The watch was all that remained of her. The only light that shone in the darkness of the hell of what I'd done.

The Old Man

Across the street was the diner. Hunger was gnawing away inside, but I thought better of the idea and walked past, headed home. Maybe I would come back later in the day after some time had passed and things had settled down.

As I walked past the old man's house, he was leaning on the gate. He stuck out his withered hand and said, "The name's Eli."

I stopped and stared at his outstretched hand for an instant, not sure what to do. I wasn't interested in who he was and certainly didn't want to be neighborly. Feeling stuck, I took his hand and said flatly, "Glad to meet you." I lied.

After an awkward pause, he continued, "And yours?"

This is what I wanted to avoid. After another awkward pause, I groped for a response. "John," I said lying for the second time, feeling uncomfortable and ready to leave. But he continued to grip my hand tightly, studying me closely.

"You got a last name, John?"

Again, I struggled for an answer. "Smith… John Smith." Might as well make it a clean sweep. I lied for the third time. It was a stupid lie, and I knew it, but it was too late to take it back. Eli just flashed that wry smile that I had seen earlier.

"Good to meet you… John Smith."

At that point, I tried to free myself by saying I needed to go, but he gripped my hand firmly.

"I've got a business proposition for you," he started out. "I've got some work that needs to be done." He motioned with his free hand toward the house. "And you need money—"

"What makes you think I need money?"

Again, he flashed that wry smile. "Well, let's see. For starters, a person who has money doesn't count what he has before ordering a cup of coffee. Then there's your recent visit to Willard's across the street. You didn't go in to buy anything because you came out empty-handed. I'd say judging from that pale band on your tanned wrist where your watch used to be, you went in to pawn your watch. But you didn't get what you had hoped for. People never do." He paused to watch my reaction. "That's how I know that you need money."

I was angry. I hated people trying to analyze me, professional therapists or prying neighbors. I hated that he was right and almost walked off. Almost told him where he could put his theories, but he was spot on. And for some reason, I liked the old man. Maybe it was because he got some sick satisfaction from what had happened in the diner. Whether it was because I was desperate for cash or because he intrigued me, I stayed.

"Well, Eli, I guess you've got me all figured out. So, what do you have in mind?"

A wide smile crossed his face. He released my hand and turning, waved toward the house again. "I haven't been fit for maintaining this place for years. You can see it needs painting and some repair." He turned back to me. "I'll pay you five dollars an hour to paint the house and replace the missing shutters." He paused, maybe because he saw the disgust on my face.

"Five dollars an hour? That's not even minimum wage." I laughed. "There's a ton of loose paint to be scraped and primed. Then there's the painting, much of it up on a ladder. You're joking, right?"

He kept smiling. "Nope, I'm serious."

I shook my head as I glanced down the road toward my little dirt lane.

Sensing that I was wavering, he spoke again. "You're approaching this all wrong. You see the glass half-empty. I, on the other hand, see the glass half-full. You need money. I need work done. We both get what we need. You get a job making five dollars an hour, which is probably the only job you'll find around here." He paused. Then with a grin, he continued, "See, the glass is half-full."

I was still wavering when I think he decided to press the issue. "Come with me. I'll show you where the tools are located." He turned and began to walk toward the house. I didn't move. He only took a few steps before looking back to see if I was with him. He stopped smiled, and motioned me toward him while calling back, "Come on, John Smith. You don't have anything better to do. Do you?"

I shook my head in disbelief. Then I followed him around to the back of the house. As I did, I passed well-kept flowerbeds of black-eyed Susans, purple coneflowers, iris, zinnias, and a variety of lilies

16

and roses. The beds were weed-free and neat. It was obvious that these flowers received equal portions of water and love. The well-manicured garden made an interesting counterpoint to the splotchy, peeling house sitting next to it. As I passed, I wondered how Eli could let the house fall into such disrepair and then devote so much attention to the flowers. He was hard to figure.

The house was as deep as it was wide. It was big, and the scope of the job was overwhelming. Behind the house, we walked past a black Lincoln Town Car. Judging from the body style, it had been a new car about ten years earlier. Despite the age of the car, it looked brand new. Just beyond the car was a long, ramshackle shed that had long since lost any remnants of paint. The wood was weathered and gray. One of the end walls bowed out causing the roof to sag on one side. The tin roof was eaten with rust. Only a few dull gray splotches of tin could be seen through the thick dark reddish-brown corrosion.

Inside, I was surprised to find a very adequate and organized set of tools. In contrast, there was a jumble of assorted cast-off items, broken or no longer used lamps, chairs, and other home goods piled in one corner. Next to these items were boxes of Christmas lights. There must have been strands of thousands of clear twinkle lights and at least a football field length of heavy-duty extension cords. Eli explained that his mother, "God rest her soul," had been an avid Christmas decorator. He, however, did not share in her enthusiasm for twinkle lights. So, here beside the other junk, they sat.

The shutters that were missing from the house were stacked neatly against the far wall. A thick layer of dust covered everything in the shed. An old, wooden extension ladder hung on the wall running the length of the shed. It was not one of the lightweight aluminum ones you find in stores today. No, this was a heavy, awkward beast. The rope that worked the extension mechanism was probably dry rotted, and I commented on my fear that the rungs might not hold weight. Eli just smiled and winked as he put his hand on the ladder. "Just because it's old doesn't mean it's useless." He lightly patted the wooden frame. "This was made in a time when quality was more important than profit. A man's character was part and parcel of what he built. You don't need to worry. It'll hold just fine." With his full, deep voice and his penchant for lecture, I wondered if he had been a preacher in an earlier life. I made a mental note, *Don't get Eli started on any subject.*

17

After giving me a brief tour of the shed, Eli headed toward the house and left me to my work. I watched as he slowly made his way, shoulders hunched, back bent, slightly limping as he shuffled away. As he rounded the side of the house, he stopped briefly to remove a few dead lily and rose blooms. His trip past the flowers was slow and halting as he stooped to gently cup a few of the blooms in his hand, lifting and admiring them like a grandparent cupping the chin of a beloved toddler. Then he was off, disappearing around the front of the house.

I stood for a moment surveying the jumble around me and regretting the mess I'd gotten myself into. But money was money. Something I didn't have much of. I gave a heavy sigh as I looked around, my gaze falling on the stack of shutters against the wall. That was it. My first task would be to take down the remaining shutters. This would make it easier to paint the house and easier to paint all the shutters at the same time. Once the painting was done, the shutters would go back up.

I hefted the heavy ladder down from the wall and laid it on the ground. Despite Eli's assurance, I checked each of the rungs and the rope. To my amazement, the old man was right. It was solid. However, I did have trouble getting the ladder to extend. Years of sitting idle in the humidity had caused the wood to swell and stick. The pulley wasn't moving either. I went back into the shed and after a moment of searching, emerged with a hammer and a can of penetrating oil. I hammered at the side of the ladder until the two wooden sections came unstuck and moved freely. Next, I doused the pulley with penetrating oil until it released and turned in my fingers.

After stuffing a couple of screwdrivers in my back pocket, I lifted the ladder and lugged it toward the front of the house. I went for the easy work first, focusing on the ground-floor windows. Then I shifted my attention to the second story. Raising the ladder and pulling the rope to extend it was an awkward challenge. But after some unsteady moments, I positioned it and then climbed up to begin. These weren't ornamental shutters. These were old school, designed to be closed to protect the windows during storms. They were mounted on sets of hinges held in place by screws. Unfortunately, each screw had been painted over numerous times in earlier years. It was also unfortunate that the screws had not been removed in a very long time. For each one,

I had to scrape away the years of paint just to find the screw head. Then I struggled to free the house's grip on each one.

I was in the middle of one of these mini battles, when a car pulled up in front of the house. I could hear the engine idling behind me. Reflected in the window, I could see a sheriff's cruiser below. I hoped unrealistically that I hadn't been noticed. Continuing to work, I pretended that I hadn't noticed the cruiser. With the heat, the strenuous nature of the work, and the added stress of the cruiser's arrival, perspiration poured down my face and seeped through my shirt. Even though I ignored the cruiser, it continued to sit and idle. I felt vulnerable high up on the ladder. There was nowhere to run and only one way out… down. Suspended there between heaven and hell, I was a dead man. Beyond the cruiser's tinted windows, I knew the deputy watched, savoring my panic before exacting his revenge.

Dead Fly in the Soup

The screen door below screeched in complaint as Eli shuffled onto the front porch. He studied the cruiser for a moment, and then moved in his labored pace down the walkway toward the idling car. I continued working on freeing a particularly nasty screw from one of the shutters and kept my head down, watching the reflection in the window. Both became more difficult as my hands began to tremble. I struggled to keep the screwdriver in the groove. As Eli approached the car, the driver's window slid down. The driver called out, "Mornin' Eli, I see you got some renovation underway."

It wasn't a voice I recognized. Not the deputy from the diner. I exhaled and felt the tension in my arms, shoulders, and back release. Losing my balance, I grabbed the ladder with both hands almost dropping the screwdriver.

Eli called back, "Yep, I thought it was time to spruce it up a bit. I could use an extra set of hands. Want to help?"

Loud laughter escaped the cruiser window before it slid up and the car pulled off. Eli watched it disappear and then looked up at me still clutching the ladder.

"You OK up there?"

I called down, "Not really. I was sure the deputy from Duke's was here to nail me."

He glanced up the road again and said, "Me too. That's why I wandered out when I saw the car."

"What was that about?" I asked, nodding in the direction of the cruiser.

Eli grinned up at me, "He was checking you out, making sure you hadn't killed me or stuffed me in the trunk of my car. We don't get many strangers in this little town. You stand out like a dead horsefly in a bowl of peanut soup."

He paused for a moment, staring up at me on the ladder. "Looks like you could use a cold beer." I realized he was commenting on the sweat that soaked my shirt and ran in streams down my face. It was a welcome suggestion, and I hurried down the ladder to take him up on his offer. Eli disappeared briefly but soon stepped out the door carrying two cold bottles. He handed me one and motioned toward the wicker chairs on the porch. He and I sat, taking long, slow sips of ice-cold beer as the sun and humidity beat down just beyond the shade of the porch. The cold liquid was refreshing. I wiped the sweat from my brow and held the cold bottle to my forehead between sips.

After a few seconds, I spoke up, "I'm a bit confused. Why didn't the deputy arrest me or at least question me about what happened at the diner?" I looked over at Eli as a big grin spread across his face. He chuckled as he offered his theory.

"My guess is that Jeb hasn't told anyone about it. The night shift here can be slow, real slow. Not much happens around here even on an exciting day. Seems like he'd had a few conversations with Sam Adams to pass the time before he arrived at Duke's." Eli paused, tilted his bottle, and took a long, slow sip. He continued, "Jeb's two outstanding characteristics are that he's mean and he's proud. I don't think he'd want the other deputies to know that he was drunk on duty, assaulted a waitress, had his gun taken from him and dumped in a coffee pot, and then was handcuffed to a stool." Eli continued to chuckle as he relived the moment.

The theory seemed sound, but I wasn't completely convinced. At any rate, I had survived my first brush with the sheriff's office.

After a moment, Eli took a deep breath and pointed at me. "So, John Smith, what brings you to this God-forsaken little town?"

I paused for a moment considering the question and the potential answers. I liked the old man, but I wasn't sure that I could trust him. My business was just that, my business. I took a long swallow of beer and then sighed, "Just drifting. No place better to go." I fell quiet having said everything and yet very little.

Eli gazed out at the sky and nodded as if he understood, but I didn't think he could. Another quiet moment passed before he asked, "Family?"

"None," That was only partly true. I had no family who'd claim me. The result was the same.

Again, the old man nodded. "How long you been drifting?"

"Fourteen, maybe fifteen months. Days all run together after a while."

"So, you haven't always been a drifter. What caused you to start?"

I studied the bottle in my hand. Raised it to my lips and chugged down the last few ounces. Setting the empty on the wicker table between our chairs, I looked up at the ladder and sighed, "Looks like it's time to finish up." I stood and began climbing the wooden rungs.

Eli took the hint. He stood, picked up the empty bottles, and called back as he moved inside, "You be careful out here in the heat, John Smith."

I thought, *How appropriate*. In the private inferno that was my life, I did need to be careful.

Dreamless Sleep

I hadn't worked this hard in a long time. My back muscles were tight, and my hands burned with blisters. The sun, now high in the sky, was a blast furnace. My only salvation was that I'd come down from the ladder and was working under the shade of the long front porch with a slight breeze blowing through. The combination of the work and the heat had the same effect as body blows to a prizefighter. After a while, they just beat you down.

I took a break around noon when Eli brought out a plate of sandwiches and more cold beer. We sat on the front porch eating and drinking. The sandwich was simple — bread, mayonnaise, country-cured ham sliced thin, cheddar cheese, lettuce, and fresh tomato. I hadn't had much to eat in the past two days. The saltiness of the ham played well against the sweetness of the juicy, ripe tomato. It tasted like the best sandwich ever.

As we ate, Eli gave me a brief history of Bethany Crossing. It seems that, during colonial times, a wealthy farmer owned most of the land in the area. On this spot, a well-traveled trail headed west intersected with another dirt road that carried travelers north and south. Over time, the farmer built a small inn where the roads intersected and named the inn after his daughter, Bethany. As the years passed, it became known as Bethany Crossing. Once a prosperous little town, it was now just one of several struggling communities in Jefferson County. This was not the most interesting lecture, but I listened carefully, relieved to be off the topic of me.

After lunch, I removed the last shutter. I was sore and tired from the earlier work on the ladder, so I decided to change things up and began scraping off loose paint. This was just as exhausting as I had envisioned, but at least I was working on the ground level. Tomorrow I would tackle the higher spots. I planned to complete one side of the house at a time. This was monotonous work and at least it would allow a little variety if I scraped, primed and then painted one side before moving to the next. It would also keep the front of the house from looking splotchy for days on end.

After six hours of climbing, hefting, and scraping, I was whipped, nothing left. I knocked on the screen door and waited for Eli. He shuffled out and down from the porch to inspect my work. He stood for a moment slowly nodding his head in approval as he scanned the front of the house.

"Well, John Smith, you're doing a fine job. A mighty fine job." He reached in his back pocket and pulled out a worn, wrinkled leather wallet, shuffled through a few bills and papers, and pulled out a twenty and two fives. "Normally, I'd wait until the end of the week, but I know that you could use the cash so here's today's pay." I held out my hand, but he came just short of laying the bills in it. With the money hovering just above my palm, he commented soberly, "Now, don't leave me with a job that's half done." He flashed that wry smile again as he placed the money in my hand.

I wasn't sure that I'd even be able to move tomorrow, but I said, "Don't worry. I'll be back to finish the job."

He smiled. "Can you be here at seven tomorrow?"

Without comment, I held up my wristwatchless arm.

He looked puzzled at first, but then a smile of realization came across his face, and he nodded. "Let me rephrase that. Can you be here early tomorrow?"

I said I could and then began to turn away.

The old man held up his hand to stop me. "Hold on." He disappeared into the house. Moments later, he returned with a sandwich in a Ziploc bag and a bottle of beer. He offered them to me saying that he figured I would need supper. I thanked him and headed toward my little dirt lane with supper in hand. I didn't quite understand what was going on with the old man, but where earlier I had nothing, I now had money in my pocket and food in hand. I would take it.

Exhausted and hot once I reached the cabin, I switched on the air conditioner. It rattled loudly as it spewed out cold air. I stripped and stepped into the shower. The water pressure was little more than a trickle of cold water, but, to me, it was a luxurious spa. After a long, slow, cold sprinkle of a shower, I put on a clean shirt and a pair of shorts. Lying down on the bed, I tried to make sense of the day. For months, I'd wandered from place to place like a man sleepwalking, numb, no emotions. Suddenly, today I felt anger and rage. In the past, other people were just things to be avoided, sometimes annoyances, but mostly flat shadows. Today, I actually found the old man to be interesting. He was prying and aggravating... but in a curious way. I wondered what his story was. Why did he latch onto me? It seemed that he found me as intriguing as I found him. Although our circumstances were very different, I suspected that we had something unseen in common.

After my sandwich-and-beer supper, I pulled one of the chairs from the cabin outside and watched as the sun slid slowly behind the trees. The fragrance of wild honeysuckle hung heavy in the air. It was just as intoxicating as when I was a boy enticed to taste its sweetness as I pulled apart the delicate flowers, touching my tongue to the drop of nectar inside. As the darkness crawled through the woods and engulfed the cabin, an ever-louder chorus of frogs and insects rose. I sat with my eyes closed as one listening to a familiar hymn. There was something calming and comforting in this loud cacophony. The concert was short-lived as the mosquitoes soon found me, and I hurried into the shelter of the cabin.

The air conditioner had done its job, and the little place was comfortably cool. I turned it off and the clattering stopped. Lying on the bed, I listened to the muffled sounds of the night. Slowly, the lullaby worked its magic. I was sure that toiling in the heat all day would lead me into a deep and dreamless sleep that would last the night. I was wrong.

The Road to Hell

I woke with a start. Springing up from the bed, I searched the darkness. Sweat ran down my face and body. I was shaking. My hands were the worst. The tremors had returned with a vengeance. My breathing came in ragged catches. The nightmares were relentless, horrible, haunting nightmares. I'd moved from place to place for over a year and still, they managed to creep through the darkness, finding me alone.

I sat for a moment, trying to compose myself. The hot, moist air clung to my body. I stumbled to the window in the darkness and switched on the clattering air conditioner. I stood for several minutes with the air blowing directly at me, trying to cool down. Then I crossed to the small bathroom, switched on the light above the sink, and looked at myself in the mirror. A haggard, disheveled, sleep deprived apparition stared back at me. There were dark, swollen circles under my eyes. My wild, unkempt hair and beard were long, ragged, and streaked with gray. How could I be so young and look so old? The man looking back at me was someone I didn't know. I looked bad.

Letting the shower run cold, I and stood in it for the longest time. After drying off, I dressed in a T-shirt and boxers and climbed into bed, hoping to return to sleep. Even as exhausted as I was, I knew it wasn't going to work. It never had before. I lay on the bed listening to the old air conditioner as it sputtered and hummed. Sleep wouldn't come. All my nightmares played out in my mind like a horror movie marathon. I needed to get busy doing something.

I rose and wandered back to the bathroom. Studying my reflection in the mirror, I ran my hand over my ragged beard. I opened the medicine cabinet. There wasn't much there but an unopened pack of pink disposable razors. Pink wasn't my color, but who would know? The Grovers in the cemetery? They were good at keeping secrets. I laid a pink razor on the edge of the sink. Unfortunately, there was no shaving cream. I closed the cabinet, studying my face again. Working in the heat would be cooler without the beard. I improvised using a bar of soap to lather my face, knowing this wouldn't be pleasant. I was right. At times the razor pulled more than cut. It felt like pliers ripping out sections of the hair. It forced me to move slowly, so it took a while. When I finished, I rinsed my face and looked in the mirror at a man I hadn't seen for a long, long time.

The faint light of sunrise filtered through the cabin windows. I didn't know what time it was, but I was sure it was "early," so I headed out the door for Eli's.

As I stepped from the dirt lane onto the highway, there was the cruiser, headed toward me. I thought to duck into the cover of the tree-lined lane but knew it would look suspicious. Instead, I shoved my hands in my pockets and walked toward the approaching cruiser, looking straight ahead as if I belonged on this road.

The cruiser slowed to a stop. The blue lights came on. The reflection of the rising sun blazed orange from the windshield making it hard to see inside. If I were lucky, this wouldn't be Jeb. The cruiser door swung open. I wasn't lucky. Out stepped Jeb, adjusting his belt as he strode toward me. This was bad, Jeb with a gun on a lonely stretch of road. I continued to walk.

He stopped and placed his hand on his holster. "Hold up, boy. I want to talk to you." The "boy" reference seemed odd since I was clearly no younger than he was.

I stopped. Thought of running again and realized it would be useless. I waited for the coming rage.

Jeb studied my face closely. "You're not from around here are you?"

I'm not sure why he asked the question. I was sure he knew everybody and their brother in this small town. He already knew the answer to the question. I wanted to smart off but held my tongue. I just shook my head.

He continued studying my face. Maybe it was this morning's shave or the previous morning's head trauma, but he seemed to be trying to put pieces of a puzzle together.

"You got any identification?"

"Yeah, in my wallet." I pointed to my back pocket and then moved my hand slowly to produce it. I pulled out my old driver's license and handed it over. It had been so long since I'd used it, I wasn't sure if it was still valid.

He looked at the license and then up at me. "Wait here."

He walked back to the cruiser. I knew he was checking for "wants and warrants." I struggled to control the tremors, my hands shoved deep in my pockets. After what seemed like an eternity, he strode back and handed over the license. A crooked grin crossed his face as I retrieved the license in my shaky grasp. I caught a hint of alcohol on his breath. Evidently, he had frequent conversations with Sam Adams when he was on the night shift.

He wasn't finished with the interrogation. "So, is that your current address on the license?"

I shook my head. "I'm renting the old Grover place."

"The old Grover place, huh?" He chuckled. He knew it was a dump, but dump or not, it kept me from being a vagrant.

"Where are you headed?"

"Going up to Eli's. He hired me to paint his house." I would have given Eli's last name, but I didn't know it. My guess was that Eli was enough for him to know where I was headed.

He was studying my face, still not sure. "Where were you yesterday between 4:00 and 5:30 am?"

I'm not sure why, but the question caught me off guard. I hesitated. Then I panicked at my hesitation. Did he notice? Maybe he finally knew, finally remembered. I tried hard to keep my voice steady. "I was in bed." I lied. It seemed to have become a common practice for me.

Jeb continued to scrutinize me. I was becoming increasingly uncomfortable. Perspiration was beading on my forehead. I clenched my hands in my pockets trying to calm the tremors.

Jeb broke the silence. "This is a quiet little town. We don't need people coming in here and stirring things up. Understand?"

I nodded, "Got it."

Jeb locked his eyes with mine to make his point. Then he turned, climbed into the cruiser, and drove off. I watched as he headed east. The sun just above the treetops and the palpable humidity created an orangish-yellow haze. It was a fireball low on the horizon with the white-hot sun in the center. The cruiser disappeared into the inferno.

I exhaled deeply and closed my eyes. There in the darkness behind my eyelids, came a haunting moment from my past.

*　　*　　*

Up close, I could smell Si's rancid breath. His black eyes narrowed, clutching mine in their grip. He growled, "Listen, new boy,

31

we're just having a conversation, a simple conversation." He paused. "We've got our own way of doing things here and we don't need some new boy coming in and stirring things up. Got it?"

I didn't respond fast enough.

He dialed up the growl a notch, "I said GOT IT?"

I spat out the answer, "Got it."

Si remained in my face for a second longer, his eyes dead on mine. Then with a twisted grin, he drew back and announced, looking around at the others, "Then we shouldn't have any problems."

*   *   *

Chilled and shivering, I opened my eyes to the present sweltering humidity. "Conversation," I snorted to myself. Simon, or "Si" as we'd called him, had the morality of a snake hunting a rodent, slithering and twisting in whatever direction necessary to make the kill.

Motionless except for the uncontrollable shivers, I gulped in the hot summer air, afraid to close my eyes again. Slowly, the shaking subsided. I took another deep breath, turned, and headed toward Eli's. The millions of tiny pieces of exposed aggregate in the worn asphalt reflected the sun behind me, giving the road an orange glow as if it were on fire. *The road to hell*, I thought. I was already soaked from the heat and humidity. It was going to be a scorcher.

Duke's

When I arrived at Eli's, I went straight to the shed where I'd put up yesterday's tools. My palms were blistered and sore. After searching for a while, I found an old set of work gloves in the shed and slipped them on. I grabbed the heavy extension ladder and the wide putty knife that I used to scrape off the peeling paint. Lugging the ladder around to the front porch, I raised it to the spot where I left off the day before. After climbing the ladder, I attacked several nasty spots of loose paint. Some came off easily, but others were just beginning to bubble and required heavy pressure. At times, the back-and-forth movement of the putty knife sounded like a saw working its way through hardwood. At times, the scraping gave off a sick squeal like nails on a chalkboard.

I must have been creating quite a racket in the house because Eli shuffled out the front door, frowning. He was barefoot and wore pajama shorts and an old T-shirt that almost swallowed him. His arms and legs were bony with loose skin hanging where muscle had once held it taught. It looked like he was being consumed from the inside out. It was later that I discovered how close to the truth I was. He scowled up at me on the ladder. "Do you know what time it is?"

Like the day before, I held up my wrist with the lily-white watchband mark.

He hung his head and shook it in disgust.

I decided to fuel the aggravation. "You said to come by early."

"Not this early."

I shrugged and he muttered, shaking his head, as he shuffled into the house.

I turned back to knocking off the old paint. Even as hot as it already was, it would be cooler to get the work done now.

About thirty minutes passed before Eli appeared at the door again. This time he was wearing a shiny pair of wingtips, dark slacks, white dress shirt open at the collar, and a tan straw hat. He looked dapper, ready for going out on the town. As he walked down the steps, he spoke without looking up, "Come on, John Smith, let's go."

It was his turn to aggravate. He would take every chance he could to jab at my fake name. As I started down the ladder, I called back, "Go? Where are we going?"

He continued down the walkway. Irritation in his voice, he said, "Just come on. These days, I move in slow motion. I'm sure you can catch up." He continued walking.

I climbed down and followed. He was right. It didn't take me long to catch up. As I drew up next to him, I gave him a long, questioning glance.

"We're going to Duke's for breakfast. I'm buying. Don't argue." His voice was gruff.

"I wasn't going to."

"Good." He shot me a sideways glance.

After a brief silence, he asked, "What happened to your face?"

"I thought it would be cooler for working outside."

A simple grunt was his reply. We walked the rest of the way in silence.

Duke's seemed the same as it had early yesterday except it was much busier now. Most of the booths and seats at the counter were taken. There was one empty booth about halfway down. The old man motioned toward it and we sat down. This time I sat facing the door, and Eli sat facing the counter of infamy. I was looking over the menu, again. Eli didn't need to.

The place seemed to serve a range of clientele. Some wore work clothes and work boots. Others were in suits. An occasional diner sported casual wear. They did, however, seem to have one thing in common. They had a strong interest in watching me. I'd look up and catch someone studying the stranger in town. Some would look away nervously when my eyes met theirs. Others would continue to stare, unconcerned that I was returning their gaze.

I heard the waitress's voice approaching from behind me. "Mornin', Eli. What can I get y'all today? The usual?"

I looked up as she arrived at the table. It was the same waitress from yesterday. She was very attractive, long dark hair pulled up in a neat bun, crystal clear hazel eyes, and that same sad smile. She wore a fitted aquamarine button-up blouse. A matching necklace with a teardrop-shaped stone hung just above the hint of cleavage visible at the open collar. Her dark khaki skirt, cinched at the waist by a wide belt, accentuated her shapely figure. She was probably what some "minus IQ" in the fashion industry euphemistically termed a "plus size," but she wore it well.

As she turned to greet a newly arriving customer, I noticed the black and blue bruising on her forearm. Finger marks were clearly visible. When she turned back, Eli pointed across the table. "Molly, this is my friend John Smith." Again, an aggravating dig. It's funny how I went from stranger, to hired hand, to friend all in twenty-four hours.

Molly looked at me and her smile faded. Her expression said, *I know this guy from somewhere.* Suddenly, her eyes grew wide. She recovered, forced a smile, and then asked for my order.

It was my turn to aggravate. "I'll have scrambled eggs, bacon, hash browns, biscuits and gravy, and a side order of pancakes."

Molly looked at me, her mouth open. "We serve big portions. Are you sure you want all of that?"

"Yep, I'm sure."

She shook her head. "OK, then."

Staring at me with a sour look on his face, Eli said, "I'll have the usual, Molly."

As the waitress turned away, I said, "Oh, is the coffee fresh brewed today?"

She turned back with a puzzled look. "It's fresh brewed every day."

"Then I'll have coffee, black."

She stared at me for a second. Then, a smile crept across her face. "Coffee, black? You sure?"

I nodded.

"OK, but it might be a bit strong." She chuckled as she walked away.

I turned back to Eli who was boring a hole in me with his eyes. "You're paying, right, Eli? I won't argue."

He mumbled, "So that's how we're going to play this game."

I smiled but as I glanced out the window at the same small town I'd wander into, I had a feeling that something was different. I wasn't sure what, but something. People, places, things—for the last couple of years, they all just blurred together, nameless, faceless. But now, Molly. I liked the name. I liked that I made her laugh. She probably didn't often have reason to laugh. I wanted her to come back to the table and laugh again. What was wrong with me?

"Something bothering you, John Smith?" Eli smirked. "Worried about running into Jeb?"

"I already did."

"What?" His eyes grew wide. "When?"

"This morning on my way to your place—he pulled over and stopped me. I could see gears spinning in his head, but he couldn't make the connection. Maybe it was the alcohol haze or the blow to the head or the clean-shaven face. Maybe it was all of them. He looked at me suspiciously, but he let me go."

A big grin crossed Eli's face as his dour mood changed. I didn't know the history between the two of them, but evidently, it wasn't good. Eli was getting too much enjoyment from this.

Molly showed up with our breakfast. She placed a plate of scrambled eggs with strips of bacon and a cup of coffee in front of Eli. Next, she placed my three plates of food on my side of the table. Next to them, she set an extra-large mug of coffee.

I looked up and she smiled, a real smile this time. She hesitated for a moment and then spoke in a quieter voice. "I want to tell you I'm sorry."

"For what?" I asked.

"The way I reacted a few minutes ago. I was a bit startled, that's all. I really am grateful for what you did yesterday."

"No apology needed."

"Well, thanks anyway. I hope y'all enjoy your breakfast."

As she walked away, I tried to convince myself that she was confused. She thought that I took down Jeb out of compassion for her. That wasn't it at all. She shouldn't apologize. She was right to be horrified. I acted out of anger, pure rage. I had dealt with cruel jerks like Jeb in the past. My patience with his kind was used up long ago.

I looked across the table at Eli who was staring at my three plates of food, shaking his head.

With a wave of my hand, I said, "Eli, would you like some?" I chuckled, "I don't think I can eat it all."

His eyes snapped up to meet mine, his stare as sharp as a knife. Then he looked down at his plate and began eating sullenly.

We finished breakfast without conversation. During our silent meal, I caught myself searching the crowded diner to catch a glimpse of Molly. I listened for her voice. I hoped to see her sad smile brighten. It never did again.

Anger

As we headed back to Eli's, I carried the large Styrofoam container with the breakfast that I couldn't finish.

As we walked, I asked about something that had been running around in my head since yesterday. "Eli, your house didn't get in bad shape overnight. It's been like this for a long time. Why haven't you hired someone to fix it before now?"

He thought for a moment, stopped, and looked me in the eye. "The right person never came along."

A bit confused, I asked, "Aren't there people around here who need the work?"

"I didn't give you the job because you needed money."

I gave him a puzzled look.

"You've got something worse than hunger gnawing away at your gut."

I didn't like where this was going. I hated being psychoanalyzed whether it was by friends, neighbors, or psychiatrists with their theories and their psychobabble.

I let the topic drop and we walked in silence the remainder of the way.

I wanted to leave and not come back, but I needed the money. Looking very put out, Eli took my leftovers to place in the refrigerator and didn't return for hours. He left me alone to take out my anger and frustration on the house – and I did.

Caution

By the time I left Eli's, I'd removed all the loose paint on the front of the house. It was ready to prime and paint. The muscles in my arms and shoulders were on fire. Even at that, I was looking forward to the switchover to painting. Eli promised that he'd have the paint ready for me in the morning and promised a surprise—something involving a change of clothes. When I gave him an inquisitive look, he held up his hand. "Just do it, OK?" Eli liked being in charge.

Carrying my breakfast leftovers and an extra thirty dollars in my pocket, I headed into town. Two blocks past Duke's was a combination gas station and mini-mart. It stood at the intersection that gave Bethany Crossing its name. The sole traffic light in the town hung in the center of the intersection, a single yellow caution light, flashing.

The mini-mart looked empty, no cars at the pumps or in the parking spaces. I stepped thankfully into the air-conditioned store. A girl sat behind the counter watching a small portable TV. I didn't recognize the show, but I could tell it was a soap opera of some sort. She looked up and, seeing me, smiled as she turned from the show.

"Hey, sugar, what can I do for you?"

She was slender with shoulder-length, bleach-blonde hair. She was maybe in her mid-twenties. Her tight, low-cut V-neck blouse and push-up bra created the illusion of cleavage, and her skinny jeans looked as if they'd been painted on her.

I glanced around the store commenting, "Just came in to pick up a few things."

She stepped out from behind the counter and flashed me a flirty smile as she passed just a little too close, saying, "I'll help you find whatever you want." I was pretty sure that she intended to walk in front of me so that I could check her out. She stopped several times to show me where the lunchmeat, the bread, the mayonnaise, and the beer were located. Each time she seemed to stand just a little too close and the store wasn't big enough to warrant a guided tour. I picked up a few things and as my arms became full, she offered to help carry them to the checkout.

Back at the register, before she started ringing up the items, she sensed that she had me captive.

"Are you the guy staying at the Grover's old place?" *Ah, small towns. Your business is everybody's business.*

I wasn't interested in conversation. I kept it simple, "Yep."

"How long you plan on being here?"

Again, I wanted to shut down the prying so I said, "Not sure."

"Well," she said as she rang up the items, "My name's Amber. Come by here anytime. I'll be glad to help you find whatever you want." Looking up, she twirled several strands of hair around her index finger and smiled. Somehow, I didn't think she was talking about the merchandise in the store.

Thanking her, I said, "I'll keep that in mind." Picking up my bag and six-pack, I pushed outside into the heat coming off the asphalt. I trudged through the late-day haze back to my little cabin home.

As I turned down the dirt lane, I was alarmed to find fresh tire tracks. Someone had driven to the cabin. Who'd go back there, and what were they looking for? The only answer that made sense was *Jeb*. He must've remembered where he'd seen me. He'd come back looking for me. He might be there waiting for me now. I tried to calm myself. Maybe I was just paranoid. Maybe someone turned down the lane by mistake. I couldn't take any chances. As I neared the cabin, I stepped into the trees and slowly made my way staying concealed by the underbrush. I reached a point where I could see the cabin without being seen. There was no car. Staying in the trees, I circled around to the front of the small clearing that held the cabin. Now, I could see the other side of the tiny building. Everything seemed OK. Finally, I felt confident enough to approach the door. It was locked, just as I had left it.

Peering through one of the windows, everything seemed to be in order. I was still unsettled but started to feel that maybe I was overreacting. I unlocked the door and stepped in, my eyes darting around warily. It was the same bleak, safe little room that I'd left earlier in the day.

I put away the items from the mini-mart and decided to eat my breakfast leftovers for supper. After eating, I dragged my chair outside and sat in the little clearing, listening to the frogs while I sipped on a bottle of beer. The clearing created a ragged oval of foliage. Above, the tree line opened to a dark sky glittering with countless stars. The moon was in a waning phase and cast less light each passing night. I stayed outside until I tired of swatting mosquitoes and then dragged my chair back inside. I should've bought mosquito repellant at the mini-mart. Maybe Amber could help me find it. I chuckled at the thought.

I drank another beer, hopeful that the alcoholic anesthesia would numb me to the evening's painful shadows. I decided to leave the air conditioner on and forego the symphony outside. As a precaution, after locking the door, I propped one of the chairs under the doorknob.

Despite the alcohol, I lay on the bed for a long time waiting for sleep to come. Eventually, it crept into my head.

Surprises

I woke, startled. What was that noise? Groggy, I searched the dark through alcohol-laden eyelids. It took a few seconds for my eyes to adjust. There was just enough light for me to make out objects. The air conditioner was sputtering and coughing. Something dark lay on the floor below it. I stumbled through the cabin and flipped the light switch. My anxiety washed away as I looked down at the front cover of the air conditioner lying on the floor. As I picked it up, I noticed that only two of the four plastic clips that held it in place were still intact. They sat on opposite corners, just enough to hold. I suspected that the vibration caused them to let go. I snapped it back in place and hoped for the best.

Slumping onto the edge of the bed, I ran my fingers through my hair. These sleepless nights were killing me. I went to the fridge and pulled out a beer. I sipped it slowly hoping that, over time, it would work its sedative magic. Surprisingly, it did and I lay down for the second time that night. Sleep came as a welcome friend, but she dressed in gowns of fitful dreams. We danced a disquieting waltz as I tossed and turned in the dark.

I woke to the sun already above the trees. Exhausted, I had slept longer than I wanted, so I hurried to get ready. Once I was dressed, I put a second set of clothes in my bag for Eli's "surprise." Whatever that was. Slinging the bag over my shoulder, I stepped out the door. Still spooked by the tire tracks from the day before, I looked carefully around the cabin before heading down the dirt lane. Snapping a low-hanging pine branch that was loaded with needles, I used it as a broom. As I came to dusty patches in the lane, I brushed away any trace of tires or footprints. It was very simple, not exactly MacGyver, but I thought that it was an ingenious way to get a fresh read on any traffic down the lane.

When I arrived at Eli's, there were several cans of primer and exterior paint sitting on the front porch. I remembered seeing an old drop cloth folded up in the shed and headed back to get it. I lifted the monster ladder on one shoulder and carried the drop cloth under the opposite arm as I headed around front, two paint brushes sticking up out of my back pocket. When I turned the corner, Eli was shuffling up the walkway from the road. He paused and folded his arms, looking up at the stripped and shutterless side of the house. His face was deeply furrowed and reflected the weariness of a restless night.

"Been out this morning?" I queried.

He nodded, still gazing at the house. "There was a newspaper and cup of coffee with my name on it at Duke's. Couldn't pass it up."

He swept one hand toward the house. "Ah, the blank canvas. I can't wait to see your masterpiece."

I didn't share his enthusiasm. To me, it was just work, hot work. I ignored his comment and spread the drop cloth, wrestled the ladder up to the side of the house, popped the lid on the primer, and stirred it. Preparation over, I headed up the ladder with the primer and a brush.

Eli stood watching as I ran the first brush stroke.

Looking down at the old man, I asked, "So what's the surprise?"

Eli had a cat-ate-the-canary smile on his face. He replied, "All in good time, John Smith. All in good time. Let me know when you're finished priming." He disappeared through the front door.

I worked through the morning, slapping primer over splotchy areas of bare wood. This was considerably easier than scraping. By early afternoon, I had all the wood covered and ready for painting. I also looked like I'd lost a paintball battle with white splatters on my arms, my face, and my clothes. The front of the house still looked splotchy, but two shades of white were better than white and bare wood.

I hammered the lid on the primer can and knocked on the front door.

"Finished?" Eli asked, as he laughingly looked me up and down. I nodded.

"I meant are you finished priming the house, not yourself."

I studied my splotchy arms and shirt with a sour look. Eli stepped out into the front yard to take it all in. He nodded his head in approval. "It's going to look real good when you're finished. Yes, sir, real good. Go ahead and clean up. We're going somewhere."

Stupidly, I asked, "Where?"

He cocked his head and gave me a you-should-know-better-than-to-ask look.

"OK, OK," I said as I gathered up the paint buckets and toted them back to the shed. Once everything was back in its proper place, I went

46

to the door and knocked again. Eli appeared and gave me the once-over. "Did you bring a change of clothes?"

Holding up my bag, I said, "Of course."

He shot back, "Of course, nothin'. You're about as stubborn and contrary as they come."

I gave him a blank stare and waited.

"Come on in. Get showered and changed. I can't take you out looking and smelling like you do."

I was a bit surprised, but I followed him into the house. The interior was in much better shape than the outside. There was a central hallway leading toward the back of the house. To the left, was a spacious sitting room with a large Victorian-style sofa along the far wall. Expensive-looking end tables sat on either side and a long coffee table sat in front of it. Nearer the door and facing the sofa were two comfortable-looking Victorian-style chairs. Heavy floral draperies hung in the windows. The colors matched and complemented the high-end upholstery of the furniture. The house had been built at a time when wooden floors were the default for construction, so hardwood floors ran throughout.

To the right of the hallway was a large office. The far wall consisted entirely of bookcases filled with neatly arranged volumes. A large mahogany desk sat, facing the doorway, in front of the wall of books. A big older model computer and monitor sat on one end. Behind the desk was a plush leather chair. The desk was neatly arranged with a leather-trimmed blotter, a leather pen and pencil holder, and mahogany file trays. Two large leather armchairs sat across from each corner of the desk. They were angled to face the person sitting behind it.

Eli led me down the hall to a stairway. "Up the stairs and to the right, you'll see a bathroom. You should find everything you need in there. We'll head out once you're dressed."

I headed up to shower. What I saw upstairs matched what I had already seen, neat and nicely furnished.

Two Women, One Problem

"Jump in," Eli called through the open window of the Lincoln, the engine idling.

"Are you going to tell me where we're going?" I asked, not moving.

"All in good time… now jump in." He smiled as the window slid up.

I hesitated a moment longer. I had a bad feeling about this, but I reached for the handle, opened the door, and slid in.

We drove for miles past fields of corn that looked drought-stunted and yellowed. After driving for some time, I asked again. "Eli, where are we going?"

He looked over at me with that wry smile of his. "We're going to Clarksville."

"Clarksville? Where the hell is Clarksville, and why the hell are we going there?"

"Now, just calm down." His voice had the same soothing, unflappable tone a parent uses with their child. This aggravated me even more.

After a long silence, he asked, "Do you know what day it is?"

"Day? What day?" I fumbled because the question came out of nowhere and because I had no reason to know.

"Yes, what day is it?"

"I don't know. Wednesday or Thursday I guess."

Eli chuckled and shook his head. "Do you even know what month it is?"

I hesitated, angry because I didn't know the answer. I knew it was either June or July. He must have sensed my frustration because he chuckled in my silence.

"Never mind, John Smith, I'll tell you." He was really starting to push my buttons. "This is July and today is not Wednesday or Thursday. Today is Saturday. You've worked enough today. We're going to Clarksville for LakeFest. You know, all work and no play…"

"LakeFest?"

"Oh yes, Clarksville bills itself as Virginia's only lakeside town. It's located on Buggs Island Lake." He glanced at me and then continued. "Every July they hold a festival. It's a big deal around here. They've got hot air balloon rides, carnival rides and games, arts and crafts, and fireworks. It's an event that draws people from all around."

This was worse than I thought, and I was held captive. The only way back was with Eli. I sat and fumed for the remainder of the trip.

As we arrived, my worst fears were confirmed. Clarksville was a frenzy of cars and people. I'd spent the past year on the far fringes of society. The last thing I wanted was to be thrown into a mass of people. Eli could see it in my face as we sat in the parking lot.

"Relax, John Smith, these people don't know you. You're just one of hundreds of strangers in the crowd." I hated his dig, but he was right. I was just another stranger in the crowd. "Come on. Put on a smile and give yourself permission to have a good time." I glared back at Eli. He turned away and chuckled, "Or not."

Eli told me that I was still "on the clock" and so he paid me for a full day of work. "Spending money," he said. With a sweep of his hand, he added, "For the festival." I grimaced. Tired and hungry, I had no intention of buying anything except supper.

Eli and I jumped on the packed shuttle in the parking lot and headed off to the festival. At the end of the shuttle ride, we waded into the tide of people that ebbed and flowed toward the "celebration." Booths were set up along the main street heading toward the lake. In all, there were about seven blocks of food vendors and exhibitors. Downtown Clarksville, like many rural towns, was in a time warp. The storefronts behind the vendor booths were straight out of the 1940s. It was like watching a colorized version of *It's a Wonderful Life*. I expected George Bailey to step out of the crowd at any moment. It was as if time stood still in this little town.

We eventually found our way to the food vendors and bought sandwiches and beer for supper. Eli motioned toward an empty picnic table. While we ate, he talked on and on about the history of the area. As I pretended to listen, I watched the flow of people streaming by, families, young couples, and older couples. Smiling and laughing, they seemed to be enjoying the whole event. I wasn't.

Finished with our meal, Eli invited me to walk the gauntlet of booths with him. I declined, choosing instead to stay seated. After a while, boredom and the dirty looks from families who wanted my table propelled me toward one of the booths to get another beer. As I stood waiting for the privilege of paying twice the price for a drink, a hand slipped inside my elbow, and I felt someone press herself against my arm. "Hey, sugar, what a pleasant surprise to see you here."

Startled, I turned to find Amber from the mini-mart hanging on to my arm. She wore a sleeveless, red and white checked, buttoned shirt that was tied just below her breasts revealing her slender torso. The shirt was unbuttoned low enough to show the cleavage created by her pushup bra. Just like our earlier encounter, her denim Daisy Duke shorts looked as if they had been painted on. She hugged my right arm with both hands.

Flipping her hair back, she smiled, "Well, what do you think about the festival? Don't you just love it?"

I felt very uncomfortable and glanced around for an exit plan. She continued to rattle on about the hot-air balloons and the carnival rides. She held on to my arm with her right hand and ran her left hand up and down my back as she chattered. I heard only bits and pieces as I searched for an excuse to leave. Just past the next booth, a scowling face glared at us disapprovingly. I knew the face but it took a few seconds to place it. It was polo shirt from my disastrous morning at the diner. The guy evidently had a serious attitude problem. I was about to tell him where he could put his attitude when I caught a glimpse of a bigger problem just over his shoulder.

Jeb's size made him stand out in the crowd as he moved through the sea of people. He was headed our way, a torpedo locked on a target. No uniform today. He wore a camouflage ball cap, camouflage T-shirt, and jeans. I knew things were about to get unpleasant. Evidently, Amber hadn't seen him coming because she was asking if I wanted to buy her a beer just as he pushed his way within earshot.

"Buy you a beer? Nobody buys my girl a drink." Jeb stepped up close enough that he could've grabbed either of us. We formed an awkward triangle.

I held my ground. I really wasn't looking for a fight, but if he forced the issue I'd hurt him. I wasn't sure which of us would catch the worst of it, but he'd wish he'd never put his hands on me. I tried to pull away from Amber, but she locked onto my arm defiantly scowling at Jeb. She railed angrily about being a grown woman and being able to choose who she would spend time with. Jeb shoved her, and she fell backward losing her grasp on me. He squared around facing me and growled over his shoulder to Amber, "I'll take care of you in a minute." She began screaming that she wasn't his girl, that he had no business talking to her that way, that he was a lying, cheating jerk. Snatching a drink from the hands of a bystander, she threw it. The cup and liquid exploded on Jeb's shoulder and back dousing him in ice and soda. His anger blew as he turned from me to Amber. Letting out a stream of profanities, he grabbed her arm and shook her like a bulldog with a rag doll.

A state trooper patrolling the crowd heard the escalating argument and rushed to intervene. Farther off, I could see a second trooper pushing his way through the crowd. It wasn't exactly what I had in mind, but this would work for an exit. While everyone focused on Jeb and Amber, I melted into the crowd and strolled over to a nearby booth to finally get my beer. The woman in front of me was intently watching the troopers as they tried to calm the heated argument. I was surprised to find that it was Molly. She was absorbed in the drama unfolding at the next booth over.

"Is Amber his girl?" My query startled her. I don't think she'd noticed that I was standing behind her. She turned and, seeing me, gave a faint smile before returning to the dying argument.

"Amber is everybody's girl." Molly's expression turned sour.

She didn't need to say anymore. As the day's entertainment dissipated, I asked, "If Jeb thinks Amber is his girl, then why did he give you such a bad time the other morning?"

Molly continued to watch the conversation, now mostly troopers talking, as she answered, "Jeb thinks *every* girl is *his* girl."

With pursed lips, she swiped at a stray tear. There must have been something between them at one time. Now, there just seemed to be anger and pain. We reached the counter and I offered to buy her a beer. She smiled, her eyes still glistening. We found a table in the late-day shade.

I studied my beer for a moment, feeling uneasy. "I want to apologize for the other morning."

Molly's eyes narrowed. "Apologize? Why?"

"Yeah, it all just happened so fast. I didn't have a plan. I left you there to deal with an angry jerk handcuffed to a stool. It couldn't have been pleasant." I looked down and fidgeted with my hands. For some reason, talking to her made me nervous. And I hate to admit it, a bit scared.

She placed her hand on mine.

I looked up to her smile.

"You stopped him from hurting me. You don't have to apologize. Jeb's a mean drunk and probably would have broken my arm if you hadn't stopped him."

She paused, eyes moist, then looked away, blinking. "I've had to deal with his violent moods for years. After he came to his senses, he was screaming and threatening." She wiped away the tears and turned with a weak smile. "I wasn't going to set him free in that condition. I called his daddy to come get him. Jeb acts tough, but when his daddy says jump, he jumps."

"That must have been a strange sight for his father, him shackled to the stool. How did you explain what happened?"

Wiping at the tears again, she said, "I didn't. He wanted to know, but I was silent. Jeb's daddy has cleaned up after him for years. He may not have known the details, but he knew from looking at my arm what happened. He probably would've pressed me for more, but he was in a rush to get Jeb out of there before any more customers came in and saw him."

She laughed through the tears. "You should've seen him trying to fish the hot keys and gun out of the coffee maker." Her laughter trailed off and she paused. "You know, his daddy never apologized. Same as usual. Clean up the mess and pretend it didn't happen." Molly's gaze was lost in the distance. At that moment, the festival and the people didn't exist. She was sitting alone in a world that only knew pain... and sorrow.

In that moment, even in her sorrow, she was beautiful. I felt for her pain and wanted to punish Jeb. I wanted to shield her from harm. I was feeling something more than anger and rage... and that surprised me.

I tried to lighten the mood. "Do you enjoy the rides here?"

It took her a second to come back from her private world. "I'm sorry. What'd you say?"

"Do you like the rides? You know, the carnival rides?"

"I don't know. I don't think they'd be much fun by yourself, so I've never been on them."

"Well, you're right. They aren't much fun alone. I want to ride, but as you can see," I swept my hands in an arc around me, "I need a partner." I stood up and held my hand out. "What d'ya say? Let's go have some fun."

I'd really gone out on a limb and was anxious when she hesitated. A mix of surprise and fright crossed her face. It was the same expression that had come over her that first morning in the diner. Had I pushed a little too hard, too fast? Slowly, a smile swept the fright away. She took my hand and stood. "They're safe, right?"

With a sober expression, I said, "Look at me. Do I look like a person who'd do anything unsafe?"

She laughed as we set off to find the rides.

Broken Down

We spent the next couple of hours hopping from ride to ride. Molly laughed and screamed as we spun around. Her laughter was infectious. For the first time in a long time, I found myself smiling... and, strangely, laughing. We rode the spinning rides over and over again. Like kids, we'd jump from one ride and race each other to the next. We rushed past bystanders, some who smiled in amazement and others who frowned in bewilderment.

I don't know if it was the dizzying movement that left us grasping tightly and yet wanting to let go. Or if it was the spinning motion, the centrifugal force pressing our bodies so closely together that I could smell the intoxicating scent of her perfume. I couldn't tell if the excitement that I felt in those moments was caused by the rush of the ride or by being swept up along with this beautiful woman. As we spun, I looked out at the crowd and caught an occasional glimpse of Eli watching and smiling.

Darkness was settling in and the blinking, colored lights of the rides lit the surrounding crowd in a wild kaleidoscope of swirling colors. Eli met us as we exited the Scrambler, a maniacal, spinning and whirling machine.

Laughing and out of breath, I called to Eli, "Want to join us?"

He grinned as he patted his chest, "I'm afraid the old ticker couldn't handle it. But you two look like you're having a great time."

I glanced at Molly who was beaming.

Winking, Eli asked, "Well, young lady, are you glad you changed your mind?"

A faint smile crept across her face. In the dark, I couldn't be certain, but I thought I could see color rise in her cheeks.

Eli smiled. "Good." He turned and looked off toward the lake. "I hate to put an end to the fun, but the fireworks are about to begin." Looking back at us, he asked, "Should we head that way?"

Molly and I looked at each other. I shrugged. "OK, Eli, lead the way."

Following a few steps behind the old man, I quizzed Molly, "Change your mind?"

A slight smile crept across her face as she looked away. "Eli stopped in at Dukes' this morning. He asked if I was coming to LakeFest." She looked forward, as we walked, still avoiding eye contact. "I told him I didn't plan on going. He kept insisting that I come. Said it would be good for me to get out."

I laughed to myself and thought, *Old man, what are you doing?*

As we approached an open area free from trees, we joined others expectantly waiting for the light show in the sky to begin.

As the sky lit up in glittering explosions and fiery, sparkling fairy dust, I looked over at Molly. She was engrossed in the moment. There was a childlike joy in her expression. She caught me staring at her, turned, smiled, and said, "Thank you."

"I'm not sure what you're thanking me for."

"For giving me a great day. I don't remember the last time that I smiled as much or laughed as hard." She held my gaze for a second and in the light of the cascading glitter, her eyes glistened. She looked away at the exploding sky, blinking back the tears. I placed my hand on her back and caressed her comfortingly.

After the grand finale, hundreds of people all converged on the shuttles. Again, it was like a sea of people ebbing and flowing as the shuttles loaded. Eli, Molly, and I rode together. Molly and I sat next to each other. I caught her reflection in the window as she wistfully looked out into the dark. The sad smile that I had seen in the diner was gone replaced by one of contentment.

Once at the parking area, we said our goodbyes. She put her hand gently on my arm and said, "Thanks again." Her head tilted slightly up as she smiled. Was it an invitation? I longed to lean in but hesitated. She turned and, in an instant, was lost in the sea of people all headed home. I stood watching, a mangle of relief and disappointment.

Eli and I found our way to his car. Luckily, because we arrived late in the day, we were parked near the entrance and were able to get out of the lot ahead of the mob of cars.

We drove home on the same winding, little country roads that brought us to Clarksville. In the dark, they seemed so much lonelier and more isolated.

Eli talked as he navigated through fields and curtains of dark trees. "Looked like you and Molly were having a good time out there today." He waited, I suspect, for me to comment. I didn't, so he talked on. "You know, I think this is the first time that I've seen you smile since I met you." He glanced sideways.

I remained silent.

He continued, "I know I haven't seen Molly laugh like she did today in a long time." He paused again.

I didn't bite.

"That girl's had a tough life. Her daddy died when she was just a little thing. Her mother raised her while working a series of low-paying jobs. Like most of the kids that grow up here, Molly wanted out of Bethany Crossing, but her mom got sick during her senior year, and her health deteriorated over the next few years. Molly started waitressing at Duke's to pay the bills and nursed her mother when she wasn't at work. Not much of a life." Eli drove on in the dark making each twist and turn as if he felt them before he even saw them.

"To make matters worse, she had a brief, unhappy relationship with Jeb that has haunted her ever since. You got a good look at that the other morning. She just can't seem to catch a break. I'm not sure why she stays here. She has a dead-end job, no relatives, and nothing holding her here." He paused, "I guess we all reach a point where we just give up."

I glanced over at Eli. The dashboard light accentuated every line and furrow in his face. He looked weary. I wasn't sure if he was talking about Molly or himself.

After a long pause, I spoke. "She seems like a good person who deserves to be happier." There was something about her that drew me to her. Maybe it was the loneliness I found in the depths of her eyes. I wasn't sure.

We drove on in silence. Eli seemed absorbed in thought. Shortly, I noticed that he was having some difficulty steering the big car and was slowing down in one of the more remote sections of road. He pulled off as far as the narrow shoulder and ditch would allow.

"Something's wrong," he muttered as we came to a stop. Eli stepped out of the car peering through the darkness at the driver's side front tire. "We've got a flat." I stepped out into the ditch and then came around the front. Sure enough, the tire was completely flat.

"Pop the trunk," I called out moving toward the back of the car. "I'll put the spare on."

Eli reached inside the cabin and pulled the release. A few minutes later, I had the spare and jack on the ground.

"Eli, when was the last time you checked the air pressure in your spare?" I was chastising more than asking.

"Don't remember ever checking it. Should I?"

My shoulders sagged as I hung my head in disbelief. "Yeah, the spare's flat too."

This was great. We were stuck in the middle of nowhere in the dark.

"I guess you'll have to call a tow truck," I suggested.

"Now, just how am I supposed to do that?"

"Your cell phone."

Eli's expression was blank.

"You do have a cell phone, right?"

A sarcastic smirk crossed his face. "No, I don't."

"Really? You're kidding, right?"

Eli glared at me.

"Great, no cell phone. I can't believe this."

Eli paused a moment for effect and then shot back, "No problem, you can call them on yours." He smirked.

I shut my mouth and fumed quietly after that.

After giving his cutting remark some time to work on me, he said, "Don't worry, John Smith. Someone will come by soon."

I shot him a hard look. Middle of the night, small rural road, what was he thinking? He must've suffered a heat stroke at the festival. We were stuck here for the rest of the night.

After about twenty minutes, we saw lights blinking and flashing briefly through the trees. Soon, a set of headlights cleared a thick stand of pines. The car slowed as it neared us and then stopped. The passenger window slid down. It was Molly. She'd been stuck in the parking lot traffic.

We filled her in on our little maintenance issue. Her smile twitched as she struggled to keep in the laughter.

"I've got my cell. Let me see if I can get a tow truck out here." Evidently, she knew someone and with one call had a truck headed out. Unfortunately, we waited another forty minutes for the truck to arrive.

We thanked her and suggested she go home, but she insisted on staying. As we waited, we talked about the festival, mostly small talk to fill the empty, quiet moments. However, the highlight of the conversation was the Jeb vs. Amber smackdown.

The tow truck eventually arrived and had an air compressor. The driver tried to inflate the spare with no luck. It wasn't until then that Eli remembered that the spare had been on the car originally, gone flat, and had been placed in the trunk to be repaired or replaced later. It seems that later never came. The car would have to be towed. Trying hard not to laugh, Molly had difficulty hiding her amusement with my visible frustration. Once the car was on the flatbed and secured, she offered to drive us home. We tried to beg off, but she wouldn't hear of it, so reluctantly we climbed into her car, Eli up front and me in the back.

As we pulled off, Eli turned to Molly and motioned with his thumb. "This city boy didn't think we would see another car all night." He chuckled and enjoyed the entertainment at my expense. Molly just smiled. As we twisted and turned along the dark country road, I occasionally caught Molly's hazel eyes glancing back at me in the mirror.

She pulled up to Eli's and let the old man out. As he opened the door, he looked back at me. "Tomorrow is the Lord's day, John Smith, a day of rest. No work tomorrow." We watched the old man as he shuffled into the big, dark, splotchy house. Molly's eyes followed him up the walkway. As he reached the door, she sighed, "I like Eli." There was a pause and then, "Most folks around here don't."

This comment caught me off guard. Molly pulled out, heading toward my place. I didn't have to tell her where to go. This was a small town. Of course, she knew where I was staying. As we approached the lane, I told her that she didn't have to drive up the lane and that I would rather walk.

"I don't mind driving you to your door," she replied, smiling back in the mirror. I didn't want her to see the ramshackle cabin I was living in, and I wanted to be sure that no surprise visitor waited at the other end. I insisted on walking. She seemed disappointed but stopped on the highway. I hesitated with my hand on the door release.

"You said that most people around here don't like Eli. Why is that?"

ELMER SEWARD

I watched her face in the mirror. Her mouth drew up in a pensive expression as if she were searching for the answer somewhere in the dark just beyond the windshield. Finally, she looked back, making eye contact. "I think most folks are intimidated by Eli."

"Eli? Intimidating?" I chuckled. Pushy, maybe, but how could this feeble, old man intimidate anyone? "I'll have to give that one some thought."

I pulled the door handle and was about to swing the door open when she called out, "Hey…"

Looking back at the mirror, I could tell she was struggling with what to say next. "John…" She said the name tentatively, unsure of what else to call me. "My shift ends at three tomorrow."

Now, she was the one who had gone out on a limb. In the mirror, I could see a mix of hope and anxiety. I liked her. We had fun together, but I was a mess. I wasn't sure that I would ever be anything other than a mess, and it wouldn't be fair to invite her into my hell. Watching her in the mirror was painful as she suffered through my hesitation. I didn't want to hurt her. "Maybe I'll see you then," I said smiling.

Her fallen smile told me that she knew "maybe" also meant "maybe not."

The corners of her mouth rose in a strained smile as she said, "OK, maybe."

I glanced at the dashboard clock, "I can't believe it's 1:15. I need to let you get some rest 'cause I know that you start your shift early."

Her voice quivering, she said, "That's OK, I don't sleep much anyway."

Her eyes were becoming misty, so I jumped out and headed down the lane to allow her to cry in private.

Lullaby

I moved carefully down the dirt lane, keeping to one side and watching the dusty spaces closely in the faint moonlight. I strained to see if my virgin dust from earlier in the day was undisturbed. I saw nothing, but in the haunting, dark shadows of the thick pine forest, I couldn't be sure. I walked slowly, listening for any unusual sound. This proved to be useless as the chorus of frogs and the rattling of the air conditioner drowned out all other noises. As I neared the clearing, I studied the open area and trees beyond. The moonlight cast a faint blue pallor over the scene. I waited and watched, swiping at mosquitoes with little effect. Everything seemed just as I had left it. Eventually, I crept around the perimeter of the clearing, making a semi-circular approach to the cabin. Moving along the back wall, I stood outside peering through the back window. It was even darker in the cabin and there was little that I could see. Finally, I worked my way around to the front and tried the door. It was locked. Fumbling with the key in my trembling hand, I unlocked the door and flipped the lights. Before stepping in, I surveyed the room. Finally convinced that all was as I left it, I exhaled with relief and stepped inside. I locked the door behind me and dragged one of the heavy chairs over to the door, jamming the chair back up and under the doorknob as a precaution.

I realized that the curtainless windows were a problem. I would need to do something about them in the morning. For the short term, I draped shirts, as best I could, to block peering eyes.

Finally, convinced that I had done everything I could to secure the little cabin, I turned off the air conditioner. I didn't want the clatter to mask any other sounds. Lying down with closed eyes, I listened to the chorus outside the cabin. Sleep didn't come easily, but slowly the lullaby of the frogs floated me off.

The Awful Price

A noise. My eyelids strained under the weight of deep sleep. A black silhouette hovered above me. I tried to move but couldn't. My wrists and ankles were shackled, held fast. I twisted and strained against what bound me, my body writhing like a snake struck with a garden spade.

From behind me, two strong hands clutched my head and held it steady. As I thrashed unsuccessfully, the figure above me slowly dragged a heavy, damp cloth over my chin, covering my mouth and letting it rest just below my eyes. He wanted to watch my rising panic and savor my fear. He was drinking in the exquisite pleasure of the dread of death. My muffled screams were lost in the darkness as I strained against my shackles with the desperation of a doomed soul.

After a horrible delay, he dragged the cloth up covering my face entirely. The second set of hands held my head immobile. And then it came. Water cascaded over my head, soaking the cloth over my mouth and nose. A long steady stream. It was like being held submerged by strong hands. The wet cloth clung to my face blocking my nose and mouth, letting only water through. I tried holding my breath, but eventually I gasped. I sucked in water, sputtered, and gagged. I felt like a person drowning.

The cloth was removed, and my breathing clattered as I coughed up water. I gasped and choked, having trouble breathing. My tormentor said nothing. This was simple torture. First, there would be the pleasure of my panic. Once he was satiated, there could only be one outcome, death. I heard water splashing into a metal bucket somewhere in the dark. The sound stopped. The hands behind me gripped my head as I struggled. The figure still hovering over me slowly pulled the wet cloth up over my face, again leaving my eyes uncovered for a moment. As the cloth slipped over my eyes, I heard his voice, "Now, you'll pay for what you did." Attempting to hold my breath, I flailed my arms and legs to the point that the shackles cut deep gouges in my wrists and ankles. Blood ran down my hands dripping onto the floor. Water filled my nose and throat. I gagged and gasped again.

No Escape

I shot up from my bed clutching my throat, laboring to breathe. Tremors shook my body and sweat ran in small streams down my face. My T-shirt and shorts were soaked. My eyes darted around the room seeking the men who had held me down and taken me to the brink of drowning. They were gone. In the daze of fright and waking, I realized that it was "the nightmare." I couldn't escape it. It was almost a nightly ritual. The vehicle of my pain and panic might vary, but there were two constants, the dark figure and his promise that I would pay for what I'd done.

I stumbled from the bed and turned on the lights. I didn't want to be in the dark any longer. Sinking onto the bed, I tried unsuccessfully to steady my breathing and the tremors that shook my body. You would think that, after two years of these constant nightmares, I would handle them better. I didn't.

Slowly, the tremors eased. I turned on the air conditioner and sat in the cold air, trying to stop the sweating. I needed to shower but dreaded the thought of water running over my head. I willed myself into the small shower stall, repeating over and over, "It was just a bad dream." The shower was brief. Quickly, I was out, drying off and getting dressed.

Eli had given me Sunday off, but as he put it when he first enlisted me, "You don't have anything better to do. Do you?" I didn't, so I readied myself for work. I fried eggs and several strips of bacon, ate quickly, and washed breakfast down with a cup of coffee. It was still very early. Just a hint of light filtered through the trees. The last time that I showed up early for work, Eli was unappreciative. I didn't want to sit in the cabin and had nothing else to do, so Eli would just have to get over it. I headed out the door.

Whisking the dust behind me with a pine branch, I moved down the lane. I chuckled at my high-tech security system. I really had to figure out something better.

Gemstones and Flowers

Back in Eli's shed, I remembered seeing an old security light in the pile of discarded items. I fished it out. The arm holding the light in place was broken and dangling uselessly from the mount. Maybe I could rig this up to the cabin to discourage nighttime visitors. I set it aside. I wasn't an electrician and figured I would have to jerry-rig it in some way. I grabbed several long outdoor extension cords from the Christmas light boxes and set them aside with the light. I searched through the drawers of screws, nails, and bolts looking for wire nuts. I found none but did find a roll of electrician's tape. I tossed it over in my growing pile. It was then that I remembered the problems with the windows. I swept the length of the shed looking for a solution. No curtains. Then I noticed several old cardboard boxes neatly broken down and tucked behind the shutters along the wall. I pulled them out and added them to my junk collection. What was I missing? I needed some way to attach things, hold things. It hit me, duct tape, the universal fix-all. I pulled a roll from the shelf above the hardware trays and tossed it on the pile. Feeling that I had a good start, I turned my attention to gathering up the paint, brushes, and ladder for the day. I would ask Eli about borrowing the pile of items later when I saw him.

This morning's work would be quieter than the morning I woke Eli. The heavy ladder banging against the house as I set it in place was the worst of it. After that, it was the smooth whoosh of brush strokes as I applied the white exterior paint. Unfortunately, this was arduous work. Although it was early, the humidity was thick, and I was swimming in perspiration. The muscles in my arms and shoulders burned from the constant back-and-forth motion, causing me to sweat even more. I needed to change up the work for a break.

I came down from the ladder and went back to the shed to spend some time on the shutters. Setting one on the bench, knocked off the loose and chalky paint with a wire brush. After several shutters, I was ready to return to the ladder. As I rounded the corner of the house, Eli was standing on the porch in the same pajama outfit I had seen the other day. He was looking up at the fresh, wet paint. He shot me a look. "You just don't listen, do you? Hardheaded, obstinate, stubborn…" His voice trailed off, running out of synonyms.

I just nodded, "Morning, Eli," and headed up the ladder. Eventually, he got tired of being ignored and disappeared into the house.

The painting and sweating, punctuated by periods of shutter scraping, continued for quite a while. Eventually, Eli appeared on the porch again. With black polished wingtips, charcoal gray suit, white, crisply pressed dress shirt, and a yellow and gray striped tie, he looked sharp. The suit seemed a bit loose on him, like most of his clothes, but he looked good. In one hand, he carried two bottles of beer. In the other he carried a bouquet of flowers that appeared to have come from his garden. He set the bottles on the wicker table.

"I'm headed off to church. I brought you something cold to drink." Holding up the bottles, he said, "From the looks of it, you've lost more fluid than this." My clothes were soaked, and my shirt clung to me.

Deciding to take a break while the beer was cold, I climbed down. Holding one cold bottle to my forehead as I sipped the other, I watched Eli shuffle off toward town, flowers in hand. As he passed through the gate, a cruiser sped by with lights flashing and siren blaring. It sped past Duke's and on past Willard's, disappearing farther down the main street. Eli stopped and peered down the road. I stepped off the porch and up to the fence next to Eli to get a better angle of view. The cruiser pulled up beside two others in the parking lot of the mini-mart. The surrounding buildings were awash in the dancing blue light from the cruisers. Jeb jumped from the car and rushed toward the side of the building. He and the other deputies all disappeared behind the store. Blue lights flickered form the other side of town and soon a state police cruiser joined the other cars. The trooper also headed toward the back of the store. A crowd of people gathered in the parking lot and across the street. A deputy strode from the back of the building and began moving the small crowd out of the parking lot.

Eli spoke over his shoulder while continuing to watch the scene unfold. "Something big. I've never seen this much commotion around here."

We watched quietly for a while and then Eli started up again. "Got to pass by there anyway. I'll let you know what I find out." I stood for a moment longer but seeing nothing new, I returned to the porch to finish my beer.

Back up on the ladder, I found my mind wandering. There wasn't much to engage it during the constant back and forth of the brush. I kept thinking about Molly. It was strange because I hadn't thought about anyone for months. It bothered me that I made her cry the night before, but I knew it was for the best. There was a good reason that I was a loner. But I couldn't stop thinking about her. I tried to focus on the paint and the brush strokes, but I heard her carnival ride laughter in the calling of the birds in the trees. I would bring myself back to the brush and bucket, but quickly I'd see her tearing eyes as she drifted off into her private world of pain. My focus continued to wander throughout the morning.

I'd made quite a bit of progress by the time Eli came shuffling back up the walkway. He stopped short of the steps, smiling broadly. "This is looking mighty good. Yes, sir, mighty good." He stood, nodding slowly in appreciation.

I looked down on his admiration, taking a needed break. "What was all of the excitement up the street?" I asked.

Eli's face clouded. "It's really strange."

"What?"

He looked back toward the mini-mart. "The girl who works at the Quick Mart was raped and murdered."

"Amber?"

Eli's gaze swung back toward me. His eyes narrowed. "You knew her?"

"Not really. She introduced herself to me and took me on a tour of the store the other day when I went in to pick up a few things."

Eli smirked as he nodded his head. I got the impression that it didn't surprise him.

"I understand that it's horrible, but why did you say that it was strange?"

Eli looked off in the direction of the mini-mart but seemed to be looking nowhere at all. "I don't know. Amber, this town, rape, murder. It just seems strange... a little off."

I didn't get it, but then I didn't need to. I waited until Eli's focus drifted back to me. As I started down the ladder, I called out, "Hey, do you have time to come back to the shed?".

His eyes narrowed as he studied me. Then he said, "I've got all the time in the world."

I led him to my little pile of collected items.

He frowned and the furrows in his brow grew deep. "Is this what you wanted me to see? A pile of junk?"

"No, I was wondering if you'd let me borrow this stuff?"

Eli looked from the pile to me with a twisted little smile. "What in the world are you going to do with this assorted collection of junk?"

"Home improvement project at the Grover place," I declared with a straight face.

He stared at the odd collection of items and then chuckled. "Take anything you like. If I wanted it, it wouldn't be in the shed." He walked off, shaking his head. He must've thought that I was really a strange bird.

I called after him, "Hey, Eli, what time is it?"

He turned, "Don't you have a—"

I held up my watchless wrist.

He looked annoyed and glanced at his watch. Then, looking up he said, "No, wait right here."

He climbed the steps and shuffled into the house. A moment later he appeared on the porch. "Come here, John Smith."

I hesitated.

He motioned me toward him. As I climbed the stairs, he said, "Hold out your hand."

Warily, I did what he asked. He dropped a small digital clock into the palm of my hand. It was blue plastic with a magnet on the back like the ones you put on your refrigerator door. On the front, above the digital display was printed "Willard's." Below was printed, "Everything You Need."

I smirked. "Gee, thanks."

As he turned away, he mumbled, "Now you can tell your own time." He disappeared through the door.

Another day or two of working for Eli and I would be able to afford to get my watch back, but for now this would do. I checked my new timepiece. It was 1:15. It seemed like a good time to knock off work. I cleaned the brush, hammered the lid on the paint, and lugged everything back to the shed. I loaded my "home improvement" items into my messenger bag along with a wire cutter, grabbed the cardboard, and headed toward the highway. As I cleared the corner of the house, there was Eli, hose in hand, watering the flower garden. He was careful not to pound the petals with the stream of water. He looked me up and down and chuckled at my eclectic load of junk hanging awkwardly from my bag.

I commented, "It makes as much sense as standing in the heat watering flowers instead of using a sprinkler."

Eli flashed that wry smile that had become so familiar. "That's where you're wrong. Sure, I could step outside for a moment and turn on a sprinkler, and I suppose it would keep the flowers alive. But they're delicate creatures. They need to be tended carefully to see that they get the nourishment they need and are protected from choking weeds. You see, flowers need more than water to flourish. They need loving care." The wry smile was gone.

Somehow, I felt that Eli was talking about much more than flowers. Beneath his sarcastic, grumpy, controlling veneer, this old man had a sensitive side. I also suspected that there was a lot more to Eli beneath that veneer.

The old man smiled as he waved at the flowerbed. "Obviously, it works."

"I'm good with the sprinkler and a few weeds."

Eli laughed, continuing his gentle watering, as I walked off toward the highway.

Along the empty road, I found myself lost in a moment from the past.

* * *

It was another summer years ago and another flower garden. We had just rented a small townhome and I'd been given the task of digging a flowerbed and planting flowers. I had to laugh at the division of labor. She picked out the flowers and designed the layout of the garden on a piece of notebook paper. I dug the bed and planted the flowers, chuckling about it as I dug. The ground was like cement and the shovel and dirt were teaming up to beat me down. I was soaking with perspiration and breathing heavily. She brought me cold beer and stood admiring my half-finished excavation. It was nothing more than chunks and clods of dirt and dust in a ragged line running halfway across the front of the townhouse. All I saw was a dusty mess, but she envisioned a garden full of colorful flowers. She smiled as she dreamed

71

of the potential. Turning to me, she threw her arms around my neck and declared, "You are my superman."

I knew my shirt was soaked with perspiration and tried to pull away saying, "Be careful. You're going to get sweaty."

She pulled herself closer, giggling, with a playful twinkle in her eye and whispered, "I hope so."

* * *

I looked off in the distance toward my dusty lane. Things were so different now. There had been a time when I loved and when I was worthy of love. There was a time when I cared. I thought, *Look at me now.*

Let the Spinner Land Where It May

Arriving at my little dirt lane, I scoured the first few feet, looking for footprints or car tracks but found none. Feeling more at ease, I walked on through the shadowy, thick cover of pine trees, emerging into the sunlit clearing. I double checked the lock and peered into the windows. Satisfied, I unlocked the door and walked into the welcome, cool air-conditioned room. I quickly showered and scrubbed to remove the paint on my arms and hands. Changing into clean, dry clothes, I felt human again.

Sitting at the table with a cold beer, I struggled with my thoughts. I held the neck of the bottle and swirled the contents, mesmerized by the spinning liquid. It reminded me of when I was a kid, playing board games with my friends. After flicking the spinner, I would hold my breath in anticipation, a mix of hope and trepidation. I willed the needle to a positive result and sometimes it worked. But, it was just as likely to turn out bad. In a way, I was sitting in this old cabin, playing the adult version. I watched the beer spin, wondering where I would land. Knowing that, despite all my "willing it," the outcome was out of my hands. In that moment, I decided to let the spinner land wherever it would. I looked at my fancy, plastic timepiece. It was 2:00 p.m. Walking out and locking the door behind me, I headed down the lane. I swept my path as I walked and threw the pine branch into the trees when I reached the highway.

I'm not sure why I showered because, by the time I reached Duke's, I was damp from the humidity again. As I pushed through the door of the dinner, I was met with the savory aromas of Sunday lunch: fried chicken, mashed potatoes, collards, cornbread, succotash, and peanut soup. It brought me back to childhood memories of Sundays at grandma's house. For a moment, I was a boy again, playing tag with my cousins in the afternoon sun as we squealed and chased each other. Or slinking off in the darkness during nighttime hide-and-seek in grandma's big backyard. Next, our legs weary, we would catch lightning bugs in the dark and watch them flash and glow in a Mason jar. Finally, we would set them free just before going inside. That was a happier time.

As I moved toward a booth, I saw Molly behind the counter. She looked weary, sad. She glanced up. I waved, and she brightened. I kept telling myself that coming to Duke's was a mistake, but myself wouldn't listen. I could still feel the touch of her reassuring hand on mine. It comforted and haunted me. It made me feel something... something I wanted to feel all the time.

Molly hurried over to the booth. "What can I get you, hun?" Her face was beaming.

"What would you recommend?"

"The fried chicken, definitely."

"Then that's what I'll have... with mashed potatoes and gravy... and some fried okra. Oh, and I'll have sweet tea to drink."

"That's all?"

I cocked my head. "Yeah, why?"

She smirked. "Just seems like you've lost your appetite after that large breakfast the other day."

We both laughed as she went to place my order. She was back in a moment with the sweet tea and a basket of hot cornbread and butter. She lowered her voice as she set the cornbread on the table and drew nearer. "I was afraid you wouldn't come."

I smiled up reassuringly, "There was never a doubt." Once again, I lied, but telling her that I struggled with the decision would only hurt her and do no good.

A broad smile swept across her face. I remember thinking that making her smile did even more for me than it did for her.

I ate my lunch quietly with Molly stopping by several times to refill my tea. Each time she smiled. It made me a bit uncomfortable. I wasn't sure where this was going, but I could tell that she had definite ideas, hopes. Now, I was starting to regret coming to Duke's, but here I was. I would let the spinner find its mark.

At three, I paid for my meal as she finished her shift. She asked me what I wanted to do as we walked out the door into the blistering heat. I was really at a loss and told her so. "OK," she said, "I'll choose."

In the daylight, her car showed more wear than I had noticed the night before. It was a Toyota something-or-other that was probably eight to ten years old. There were small dents along the passenger side.

The white paint was dull and chalky. Several pitted areas around the wheel wells were beginning to eat away at the metal. As I climbed into the passenger seat, I noticed that the interior had aged much more gently. Molly swung out of Duke's lot, up past the mini-mart. As she did, she commented, "Isn't what happened to Amber just awful?"

I nodded. "Yeah, hard to understand."

"You know, Amber and I were never best friends, but she didn't deserve what she got. It's a real shocker. Nothing like this has happened around here as long as I can remember." There was a long moment of silence. I could tell that she was struggling to understand the whole thing. "I hope they catch the monster who did it." Her face was stern. She was probably contemplating what horrible things should happen to the murderer.

Molly wanted to change from her work clothes, so we were stopping at her place first. We drove for about a half-mile. Molly swung the car into a long gravel driveway. There was a cozy little rancher, probably two or three bedrooms and a detached two-car garage.

"Nice house," I commented as we pulled up the drive.

Glancing over, Molly smiled, "I don't live in the house. I rent the apartment above the garage."

I regretted my comment, but Molly didn't seem to be fazed by it. I guess she'd made peace with her living arrangements a long time ago. She pulled her car up behind the garage where a long stairway ran up the back to a small landing and the entrance into the upstairs apartment.

Motioning toward the sofa, Molly invited me to have a seat while she changed. She disappeared into what was probably the bedroom as I sat down. The apartment was small but neat. It appeared that the upstairs had been divided into two areas. One was the living room/dining room/kitchen. I sat in this area. There was a deep red sofa on one wall and a small kitchen counter with sink, white stove, and white refrigerator running along the opposite wall. White cabinets ran below and above the kitchen counter. A portable TV sat on the counter in the far corner. In the center of the room was a small rectangular wooden table with a wooden chair at each end.

There were dormer windows just above the sofa and opposite just above the sink. Faded rose floral print curtains hung in both windows. The furniture and appliances appeared to be clean, neat, but old and worn.

After a few moments, Molly appeared wearing a pair of khaki shorts and a turquoise V-neck knit top that fit her like a glove. Turquoise earrings and a matching necklace completed the look. She was a striking woman, tall and shapely. The shorts weren't too tight or too short, but they heightened the effect of her long legs. She was understatedly sexy. I found that I was attracted to her on a physical level as well as an emotional level. This wasn't good. I was just trouble, and from what I could see, she didn't need more of that.

"All ready," she smiled and spun as if modeling the outfit.

"OK," I said. "Where are we going?"

"It's a surprise. It's a place I loved as a kid, but I haven't been able to go there in quite a while. It's nothing grand, but it will be a real treat for me, courtesy of you."

That comment escaped me completely. It must have showed because she just laughed and with a flip of her hand she said, "Don't worry. You'll see."

She pulled a small cooler from the kitchen cabinets. She then placed cold drinks from the refrigerator in the cooler and dumped in ice from the freezer. We were off with cooler in hand.

I commented on how nice her apartment was. She just shrugged. "I can't take any credit. It's a furnished apartment. None of it belongs to me, not the furniture, not the appliances, not even the curtains – all belong to the family I rent from."

I nodded. "Well, I still like it."

She smiled.

We drove back past Duke's, past Eli's, and headed out of town. Molly had a childlike twinkle in her eyes and, to my surprise, turned off the highway.

Memories

Molly swung the car onto the dirt lane that led to my little cabin. I glanced over. She cut her eyes toward me with a coy smile. Pulling up in front of the cabin, she turned to me and announced with a sweep of her hand, "This is where I grew up, my childhood home." She seemed almost giddy.

I sat in the car for a moment as she opened the door, stood, and slowly drank in the surroundings like a person parched from thirst. She took a deep breath and exhaled slowly, savoring the moment. She caught my gaze with a twinkle in her eyes.

"I want to ask you for something, but it's OK to say no. I'll understand." She paused seeming reluctant to ask the question.

It made me anxious, but I offered, "Ask away."

Molly hesitated. Her smile faded. "Could I go inside my old house?"

I felt a wave of relief. I had imagined much worse. Grinning, I said, "Of course. It's a bit messy, but if you don't mind—"

"No, no, no. I don't mind at all."

I unlocked the door and let her in. She stood near the center of the room slowly taking it all in. She ran her hands lightly over the wooden chairs with a wistful smile. She wasn't really there with me. She was off in her childhood, reliving moments. Perhaps a time when she had peeled potatoes and carrots, cutting them for her mother as she made soup. Or maybe a time when her mother lovingly stood beside her at the small stove, teaching her how to slowly add flour and stir to make a roux. Maybe she was remembering hours spent with her dolls or playing games on the floor. Watching her engulfed in her memories, it struck me how strongly perspective colors our lives. We stood in the same room at the same moment. I saw a run down, cramped, old cabin. She saw a home where there was love, joy… and, in the end, the sadness of loss. I stood silently as memory after memory washed over her. Eventually, she placed her hand gently on my arm, smiled, her eyes moist, and said quietly, "Thank you." She walked out the door turning briefly to look back. I followed. Outside, she took a deep breath and exhaled trying to recover. She wiped tears away, fanned her face with her hands, and then smiled at me again.

I swept my hand toward the small family cemetery. "So, this is your family?"

Still wiping away tears, she walked toward the headstones. "Yes, this is my mother." She was standing in front of Martha Grover's marker. She then started mashing down tall weeds next to the headstone to reveal an even smaller stone marker. "This is my father." The marker simply read

Joshua Grover

1954-1992

In a poor attempt at humor, I asked, "So you brought me here to meet your parents?"

As soon as I had spoken, I regretted it. Molly's face flushed and she stammered, "Well, I hadn't really thought of it that way."

I apologized and told her that I was trying to be funny, but I could see that she was still a bit thrown by my comment. I needed to change the subject. "So, what did you do for fun when you were a kid living here?"

Molly looked off into the trees. A smile crept across her face. "I used to play in the woods. I had great adventures. There were no other children nearby, so I had to use my imagination." She stopped and turned to me with wide eyes. "Want to see my secret castle? It might still be there."

"Sure, where is it?"

Molly began tramping through the underbrush just past the cemetery. She fought her way through the shrubs and vines. As she made her way, she looked back and motioned to me. "Come on. It's this way."

I followed.

We hadn't gone far before the underbrush and trees made it impossible to see the cabin behind us. Finally, she stopped, looking carefully at the thick tangle of foliage in front of us. Then with childlike excitement she shouted, "There it is!" I blinked and looked around. I didn't see anything. At first I thought it was truly an imaginary castle. I was only partly right. A big oak tree stood before us. Molly approached the tree, stooped down, and then disappeared inside a covering of vines and underbrush. I walked around to where she had disappeared and saw that there was a small hut constructed of bent tree limbs forming an arch. The whole structure had been swallowed up and camouflaged by the forest, but the structure was solid, and Molly was crouched inside.

"Very impressive," I commented. "How did you find it? I couldn't see it, and I was looking right at it."

Molly crawled out. Brushing her hands together to remove the dirt and leaves, she said, "It's really simple. You go in a straight line from the house through the headstones until you see this oak tree. The trees around here are mostly pine. This is the only big oak around here."

I looked back nervously at the now invisible cabin and said, "That makes sense, but how do you find your way back?"

Molly could see my concern and smiled. She pointed back in the general direction of the cabin. "Do you see the two pine trees that look like they're growing out of the same trunk? They form a V shape."

I looked and, sure enough, there were two tall pines that looked like a V.

"You head for that V and keep going straight. The house will soon come into view. If you miss, you'll either come to the lane or the highway and you can just double back from there." She smiled, seeming very pleased with herself. I think that she noticed my relief to have some direction. She started off and called back, "Come on. Let's get back. I've got more to show you." Again, she led, and I followed.

Troubled Waters

We emerged from the trees right at the little cemetery. I was amazed. Molly pulled the cooler from the car and continued walking past the cabin, calling back, "Come on." When I reached the back of the cabin, Molly was waiting. She pointed into the trees just beyond. "The trail is still here. I wasn't sure it would be."

I'd never noticed it before, but there was a narrow path, overgrown in places, leading into the trees. Molly started down the trail with me following once again. After walking a short time, I noticed what sounded like the splashing and gurgling of water. As we walked, the sound grew louder. Soon, I could glimpse patches of water through the dense underbrush. We cleared the trees at the bank of a small stream.

Molly looked up and down the bank searching for something. Attracted to a large clump of high weeds by the side of the creek, she began digging through them with her hands. She called out, "Give me a hand." I wasn't sure what she was doing, much less how I could help, but I stepped up beside her. I could see that she was uncovering something green and smooth. I started pulling back the weeds and underbrush that covered it. As we worked, it became apparent that it was the hull of some type of boat. More work revealed that it was a canoe flipped upside down in the weeds. After a bit more work, we were able to free it from the grasp of the creek bank weeds. Molly grabbed one end and told me to grab the other and flip it over.

Mud fell from the sides, and bugs scattered as we turned the canoe upright. It was obvious this was home for a variety of insects. There were two wooden oars mashed into the mud below where the canoe had rested. They were gray and weathered. Molly scooped them up out of the muck and dipped them into the creek to wash away the mud.

Looking over the hull of the canoe, she announced. "I think it's still in one piece. Let's give it a try." Memories of the nightmare were still fresh, and I wasn't crazy about being anywhere near water, but I pressed on grasping the canoe tightly to subdue the tremors that were playing havoc with my hands.

We dragged the canoe over to a flat area of the bank and partly into the water. I helped Molly as she stepped into the canoe and moved to the other end. The cooler went in next. Pushing the canoe into the water, I jumped in as it cleared the bank. We slid along the water like butter gliding across a hot griddle. Molly sat in the bow, and I sat behind her. She pointed downstream saying, "Let's go this way." We slowly plunged our oars into the water in unison. I could hear the splash of the oars as we pushed ahead.

As we navigated the small creek, Molly took in a deep breath and exhaled slowly, "I love this place. When I was young, I spent a lot of time out on this creek." She glanced over her shoulder and smiled at me. "I know it's silly, but I imagined myself floating downstream past large, old plantation homes, towns and large cities with tall buildings gleaming in the sunlight, large ships carrying passengers to faraway lands, golden beaches and then into the deep, crystal blue ocean." She was no longer paddling but looked off into the distance as if she could see her childhood dreams just beyond the bend in the creek downstream. I stopped paddling as well.

Molly turned in her seat to face me. My continued discomfort must have been visible because she asked if I was all right. I nodded. "Water makes me a bit uncomfortable. I know some people who've had bad experiences." She nodded knowingly, but I don't think she could fathom the depth of the fear.

She related the story of a friend who nearly drowned while fishing. "She was never able to go out in a boat after that. For her, water became something dark and sinister."

I could see her struggling with this last statement and then she spoke, "Isn't it funny how the water led me to dreams of travel, golden sandy beaches, and the deep blue ocean, and water led her to nightmares of drowning and death?" I could tell that this contradiction had never crossed her mind before, and she was still trying to grasp it. She stared over the edge of the canoe at her own reflection in the rippling water and then it struck her. "It's not the water that's good or evil. It simply reflects our inner dreams, wonderful or dreadful." There was a moment of silence and then Molly spoke, but she was back in our world. "When I was a child, this stream was a magical path to far off adventure. Now, when I look at it, all I see is a brown and murky creek. I guess dreams are for children."

Reflecting on last night, I knew that my dreams weren't for children… or adults. She was quietly lost in her reflection in the water with a heavy sadness on her face. Despite her solemn look, I saw the sunlight dancing in the ripples of her reflection giving her a glittering beauty. She was gorgeous, and I felt myself being drawn to her by an unheard siren's song. These were dangerous waters and I told myself to resist with little success.

After a long silence, Molly looked up with a sad smile and asked if I wanted something to drink. I nodded and she opened the cooler. Handing me a cold beer, she took one out for herself. We sat in silence, taking long sips of the cold liquid.

Finally, I spoke up. "You seem to miss this place."

Her smile brightened. "I miss the great times I had here. I wish that I'd been able to keep the house and the land, but when I was in high school, my mother was diagnosed with cancer. At first, we hoped that the surgery and chemo would cure her, but it turned into an endless cycle over several years. We couldn't afford the medical bills. Although we got a lot of help with them, I had to sell the place to pay the remainder of the bills after she passed." At this point, I could see her eyes beginning to tear up. "Some group up around Richmond wanted the land to build a hunting resort or something like that. Not sure what happened, but it never got off the ground. They just recently started to rent it out. I guess they're trying to keep from losing more money on it. Word is that they're trying to sell it." She was now wiping away tears from her eyes. She put on a smile and said, "Thanks for letting me come and relive my childhood."

I smiled, "You're always welcome here. This is really your home."

Molly's smile brightened again.

After an awkward moment, she exclaimed, "Where are my manners. All we've done is talk about me."

I became uncomfortable. "I really don't like talking about myself. There isn't much interesting to say," I replied.

Molly laughed, "I don't believe that. I've never been anywhere, but I'll bet you've been to some interesting places." She waited for a response. After a moment, she put on a cheesy smile and shrugged, trying to prompt me.

I frowned. "No place special. Mostly small towns like this." I didn't want to go down this road very far, so I hoped the answer would take us to a nice dead end.

She was looking off down the creek. "I've always wondered what it would be like to travel to exciting places. You know, England, France, maybe the Caribbean…" Her voice trailed off as she became lost in her dreams. She quickly recovered, looked up at me, smiled and apologized. "Sorry, there I go talking about me again. How about you? Ever been to another country?"

"No," I responded. I didn't like lying to her, but I could already feel my fingers beginning to twitch. I laid the paddle across my lap and grasped it tightly with both hands trying to mask the beginnings of the tremors.

I'm not sure if she sensed that I was lying or caught the tension in my voice, but she dropped the subject. Instead, she commented on how dreaming of travel was just a silly idea and how she should just be happy to be out on the water on a sunny day.

By this time, we had drifted downstream a bit. Molly evidently was finished with canoeing because she suggested that we paddle back to where we launched. In a few minutes, we had the canoe back on solid ground, and I was feeling a bit more at ease. There was a large fallen tree just up the bank. We carried the cooler up and sat next to each other on the almost horizontal trunk. Other than the carnival rides, this was the closest that the two of us had been. I caught a faint hint of perfume, a very subtle floral scent like gardenia. Her hair was pulled up in a bun, but several long, dark strands had come undone and draped across her face just over one eye like a teasing veil. In the sunlight, her hazel eyes were brilliant fireworks of green and gold. She was strikingly beautiful. We sat and watched the water splashing by as the sunlight danced on the surface.

I broke the awkward silence. "You said something the other night that I didn't quite understand. When we dropped off Eli, you said that most people around here don't like him. The reason you gave is the most puzzling piece. You said that they're intimidated by him. How can an old man like Eli intimidate anyone?"

She smirked, "Well, Eli was born and raised here. He got a scholarship to a top college, graduated with honors, and went on to a very successful career in northern Virginia. The few who leave here and become successful never come back, but here's Eli, educated, successful, enough money to live comfortably right in the middle of those of us who never made it out. He's a kind, down-to-earth man. Doesn't put on any airs, but folks are still intimidated."

I considered what she said and then asked, "If most people who leave don't come back, why did Eli?"

Molly smiled. "Even with all his success, his marriage fell apart. After years of being married to his high school sweetheart, there was a nasty divorce. She moved back here to live with her family. He stayed up north. Folks say that the next thing to fall apart was Eli's successful career. After several years, he retired and moved back. Her family hates him and, except for a few distant cousins, his family has passed on. He lives like a hermit in that big, old house. Several times a week he comes by the diner very early."

"Like the other morning?"

Molly nodded. "I don't think he sleeps well. Each time that he comes in is the same. He orders two eggs over easy, two strips of bacon, and a cup of coffee. He spends a few minutes looking over the newspaper, and then nurses the cup of coffee for an hour or so looking weary, almost sad." A faint smile crept across Molly's face.

"He usually comes in before the day's newspaper arrives, so he ends up with someone's cast-off paper from the day before. One time I pointed out that he was reading yesterday's obituaries. Without blinking, he commented, 'They're just as dead today as they were yesterday.'" Molly chuckled, "And then he said, 'It's just as well. It gives me an extra day before I see the news.' When I asked what news, he grinned slyly, tapped his finger on the obituary page, and said, 'The news that I didn't make it through the night.'"

I smiled at Eli's gallows humor. Then I questioned Molly. "You said he doesn't really have family here. How about his former wife's family? Do many of them live nearby?"

Molly nodded, "They're all over the county, cousins, nephews, and nieces."

I looked at her questioningly. "Why would he move back here if he had no family to speak of and there were so many people here who hated him?"

"I've never asked and he's never said, but folks believe that he came back to be near her."

I shook my head. "I'm not so sure. I think he has a lady friend. I saw him leave with a bouquet of flowers this morning on his way to church."

Molly smiled, "Every Sunday, spring through the fall, he places a bouquet of flowers on her grave in the church cemetery. He then attends service with people who would rather see him laid to rest in that same cemetery. It can't be easy, but every Sunday he takes flowers to the woman he still loves."

She paused as she let the last sentence sink in. My admiration for Eli grew, so did my disappointment with myself.

Molly continued, "I think Eli likes you. I've seen him smile in the past few days. That's something very rare. And him at the LakeFest? He never goes to things like that." Her eyes narrowed. "He dragged you to it, didn't he?"

I nodded.

She smiled and shook her head. "Yep, he likes you." She looked away for a moment, then shifted her gaze and her eyes met mine. "I like you too." She tilted her head slightly, tossing the dark strand of hair just past her eye so that she could see me clearly. "You're the only person in a long time who has treated me like I matter."

At that moment, we were close, too close. Her wide eyes were emeralds set in gold, sparkling. I leaned in, my lips finding hers. The kiss was slow and tender. She reached up and touched my cheek with her hand. I felt a stirring inside that had long been dead.

Suddenly, there were muffled shouts coming from the direction of the cabin. We both pulled away startled. We looked back in the direction of the voices, but it was impossible to see through the thick underbrush. Molly and I exchanged glances, unsure of what to do. Reluctantly, I said, "We better find out what's going on."

As we closed in on the cabin, I got a sinking feeling. I could only get glimpses through the thick foliage, but it looked like there were cars, not Molly's, parked near the cabin. As we emerged from the small path, we startled a deputy with his gun drawn. He spun toward us and yelled, "Hands up where I can see them."

Molly jumped as she shrieked, "Cooper, put that gun down!"

Cooper kept his gun trained on me and commanded, "Molly, step away... STEP AWAY!"

Molly moved a few steps to the side. Just then, Jeb and another deputy rounded the corner of the cabin, each with his gun drawn. They spread out to cover me.

Jeb yelled out, "Molly, get over behind the cars." She hesitated. "MOVE NOW!" She backed toward the cars continuing to watch the drama play out.

She sobbed, "Jeb, what're you doing?"

Jeb ignored her. Still with his gun trained on me he shouted, "You, put your hands up… higher! Now, turn around slowly. Keep your hands where we can see them!"

I complied.

"Now, spread your feet apart… farther!" Again, Jeb barked, "OK, place your hands behind your back, wrists together, palms facing outward."

Again, I complied.

From behind, Jeb slapped handcuffs on me while the other deputies covered from the back two sides. He squeezed the cuffs to the point that they bit into my wrists. Next, he searched me for weapons. He found none.

Jeb was now very business-like. "Joseph Pittman, you are under arrest for the murder of Amber Purdy. You have the right to remain silent…" I stopped listening. I was familiar with this drill. I didn't kill Amber, and I certainly wasn't going to tell them anything. I was innocent, but opening your mouth in an interrogation was like opening wide for the dentist. The result was sure to be painful.

Jeb led me to one of the cruisers, roughly pushing me along. At the door, instead of guiding my head safely into the car, he bounced my head into the top of the doorframe. It made me dizzy for a moment, and I could feel the side of my head swelling. As he was closing the door, he leaned down and whispered, "You're gonna' pay, boy." He slammed the door and walked around to the driver's side. Just before he slid into the car, he pointed at Molly and barked, "I'll deal with you later!"

As we drove off, Molly stood beside her car, still crying. She had the same look of shock and horror that I saw that first morning in the diner.

Who is John Smith?

The county sheriff's office was an old, brick building that sat next to the courthouse. The courthouse was a two story, wooden structure painted white with Roman columns across a wide portico and a broad brick stairway leading up to the entrance, a popular architectural feature in southern courthouses. In contrast, the sheriff's office was a squat, box-like structure. There were glass doors leading into the main entrance. Extending from the rear of the building, tucked out of public view, was a wing of cells with barred windows. We parked in the rear of the building, and I was led in through a heavy metal door and placed in a small holding cell, three cinderblock walls with a small metal seat built into one corner. The fourth wall was a barred view of a large open area with office cubicles and desks. A couple of uniformed deputies sat at computers. As employees came and went, they all peered into the cell to see the caged animal. Eventually, I was taken for fingerprinting and a mug shot. Then I was returned to the holding cell.

As I sat watching the office bustle and the curious passersby, Jeb strode up to the cell. He stood for several seconds. His face was stern, his eyes as black as a moonless night. Someone called his name from across the room. He didn't respond. He stood several seconds longer for effect and then walked off toward the voice that called him again.

I lost track of time, but after what seemed like forever, I was led to a sparse office. Along one wall was a desk and office chair. A dinosaur of a computer sat on the desk. There were a couple of framed certificates on the wall behind it. Along the opposite wall ran a small table with four chairs. Two of the chairs were occupied. In one, sat a large, uniformed man. Unlike the deputies who wore all brown uniforms, he wore brown uniform trousers and a white shirt. His salt and pepper hair was cropped short. Although he was large, he appeared to be solid. The other man wore a dress shirt and tie. He was much younger, perhaps in his early to mid-thirties. He was leaner but not slender. A legal pad sat before him on the table. The deputy named Cooper led me to one of the empty chairs. Once I was seated, Cooper stepped back but hovered behind me.

The younger man spoke, "I'm Detective Hardaway and this," he said pointing to the older guy, "is Sheriff Barksdale." He looked beyond me and asked, "Has he been given his Miranda rights?"

From behind me, Cooper indicated that I had.

The younger man spoke again, "Do you go by Joseph or Joe?"

I said nothing. He waited for a couple of seconds and then started up again as if unfazed. "Well then, we'll call you Joe. You're here, Joe, because you are charged with the murder of Amber Purdy." He picked up a pen and slid his pad into position. "Did you know Miss Purdy?"

Again, I said nothing.

"Look, Joe." He tried to take on the tone of a friend giving advice. "Things will go better for you if you cooperate. Maybe there's a good reason that you're here right now. You need to help us understand."

He paused for a moment to see if the soft approach was going to work. Just as he was about to speak again, there was a knock at the door. Another deputy stuck his head in and said, "His attorney's here."

The detective stopped, his mouth open to speak, a confused look on his face. The sheriff barked, "His what?"

"His attorney, sir," came the response from the door.

I was trying not to show it, but I was just as dumbfounded as they were. I didn't have an attorney, at least not one in Virginia. It had been over a year since I'd talked with the one in North Carolina.

The two men at the table exchanged uncertain glances. The sheriff scowled toward the door. There was an awkward, empty moment. Eventually, the detective said, "Bring him in."

I swiveled in my chair so that I could see the door. It opened and in shuffled Eli, dapper as ever in his suit and tie. In one hand was a worn leather portfolio. As he approached the table he spoke rather sternly. "Evening, gentlemen. I hope you haven't been questioning my client without his attorney present. That would be highly inappropriate." He stood by the empty chair, staring each man down for a few seconds.

The detective stammered, "He didn't tell us he had an attorney."

Eli's face contorted in fake surprise. "Really?" He looked at me and then at the two men. "It must have slipped his mind." At that point, Eli sat down in the empty chair.

The sheriff growled. "I thought you were retired."

A slow grin crept across Eli's face. "Semi-retired, Sheriff. A man has to stay busy, you know." There was a moment's pause, and then Eli started up. "So, why have you gentlemen detained my client?" As he spoke, he opened his portfolio, pulled a pen from the inside suit-coat pocket and paused, looking up, prepared to write.

The sheriff took over at this point. "Your boy, here, has quite a reputation. We spoke with a detective down near Fayetteville. Seems he's had a number of scrapes with the law down there. Several drunk and disorderlies, a DUI... oh, and I almost forgot, arrested for murdering his wife."

"The charges were dropped!" I shouted as I attempted to stand. Cooper shoved me back into the chair. Eli held up his hand to calm me. The sheriff was baiting me, and I knew it, but I flew off without thinking. I glowered at him from my seat.

The sheriff shot back, "That doesn't mean you didn't kill her. They couldn't make it stick because their witness disappeared. You probably killed him too." He hoped to get me going again. He was the sadistically smiling dentist, drill in hand, just waiting for me to open my mouth again.

Eli stepped in like a referee breaking a clinch in a prizefight. He put down his pen and leveled his gaze at the sheriff. "Jim, you know that none of that is relevant to the matter at hand."

"Not relevant?" The sheriff's volume was escalating. "There is nothing more relevant. Your boy has a violent past. He was seen flirting with Amber just hours before she was sexually assaulted and murdered, and his fingerprints are on the murder weapon! It's all relevant."

The sheriff had worked himself up, but Eli locked in, returning his stare. "From what I understand, the state troopers had to break up a heated argument between your son and Amber just hours before she was murdered." Eli held his gaze and held his ground.

The sheriff's son? Arguing with Amber? Then came the realization, Jeb was the sheriff's son. Of course. That's how daddy was able to clean up his messes. Probably how Jeb was able to keep his job despite his out-of-bounds behavior.

Now, Eli was playing the sheriff, sending his anger spiraling. The sheriff jabbed his finger in my direction. "HE murdered Amber Purdy. HE tried to rape her. When she resisted, he slit her throat. His fingerprints are all over the murder weapon." The sheriff had a confident grin on his face as if he had just slammed the cell door shut on both Eli and me.

"Is that so? Let me guess. The murder weapon was a pocketknife, about a three-inch blade, black plastic handle, part of the plastic missing on one side. The kind that has studs on both sides of the blade to make it easier to open with either hand." Now, Eli was smiling.

The sheriff sat, mouth open, speechless for a moment. "How… how did you know that? We haven't released that information."

I glanced at Eli and was speechless as well. He had just described my pocketknife, but I couldn't remember ever showing it to him.

Eli continued to smile, "We'll get to that in just a moment. Now, what did the medical examiner estimate as the time of death?"

The sheriff glared at Eli. After a moment, the detective spoke. "The medical examiner estimates the time of death between 10:00 p.m. and midnight."

Eli nodded as he jotted a few notes on his pad. He looked up, "Can I see the crime scene photos?"

The sheriff had recovered and jumped in, "You'll have to wait for discovery to look at the evidence."

Eli laid down his pen. His eyes narrowed. His voice was firm, slow, and measured. "You have arrested my client. If this arrest isn't solid and you knowingly keep my client in custody, you're going to have a problem. I can tell you already from the information you've given me that this arrest is shaky. Now, where are the crime scene photos?"

The detective gave a questioning look to the sheriff, waited a second, then asked, "Jim?" I got the impression that there had probably been a difference of opinion on how to handle this investigation from the beginning. The detective asked again, "Jim?"

Eli spread his hands. "Well, if you're afraid—"

"Afraid?" The sheriff snorted, "Wasn't afraid of you ten years ago and not afraid of you now."

"You should have been."

"Ha. You lost that case then and you're going to lose this one too."

"A witness gone missing, probably dead. Is that what you call losing?"

The sheriff laughed, "Result's the same."

I thought I saw a flicker of anger in Eli's eyes, but then he smiled. "Well then, if you're not afraid, there's no reason to keep the photos from me."

The sheriff drummed his fingers on the table for a second. "He's going to see them eventually anyway. Won't make any difference. The boy's guilty. Let him have a look."

The detective retrieved a manila envelope from his desk, returned to the table, and slid it to Eli. He removed the photos and studied each one carefully making a few notes as he did. From my seat, the pictures were mostly visible. There were pictures of Amber's naked, contorted body on the asphalt behind the mini-mart, a nasty gash running across her throat. There were also pictures of her blood-soaked clothes strewn on the asphalt.

Eli placed the pictures back in the envelope and slid it back to the detective.

He looked down at his notes and then back up alternately between the sheriff and the detective. "Let me get this straight. You believe that my client sexually assaulted Amber and then killed her."

The sheriff said, "That's not what I 'believe.' That's what happened."

"Well, there are several problems with your theory." Eli gave his signature wry smile. "In the photos, her clothes are soaked in blood. This tells me that she was fully dressed at the time that she was killed. The clothes were removed later, probably to make it look like a sexual assault. Next, there is very little blood around the body. If Amber had been killed at the mini-mart, those wounds would have resulted in much more blood on the ground. She was killed somewhere else and dumped there to be found. My client doesn't have a vehicle."

The sheriff blurted out, "He could have stolen a car and dumped her there."

Eli stared him down. "Have any vehicles been reported stolen?"

The sheriff was silent.

"With all the wooded area around, why would someone kill and dump the body in the open? The logical answer is that they wanted the body to be found." Eli stopped to let this information sink in.

"The next problem with your theory is the time of death. My client was with Molly Grover and me until 1:00 am on the night that Amber was killed. I drove him to LakeFest that day and we had a flat tire on the way home. Molly saw us on the side of the road, stopped and waited with us for a tow truck, and then drove us home. We didn't arrive back here until 1:00 a.m. You can corroborate my story with her if you like." Again, Eli waited for a reaction. The detective played nervously with his pen, looking down at his pad. The sheriff's eyes were piercing as he stared down Eli.

"The last issue with this arrest is the murder weapon. The reason I was able to describe it in detail is because my client dropped it, along with a number of other items, on the floor at Duke's last Thursday morning. He accidentally kicked it away as he was scrambling to pick everything up. He evidently didn't see it because it was still on the floor, several feet away, when he left."

The sheriff looked incredulous. "Your client left his knife on the floor, and you didn't tell him?"

Eli smirked, "He wasn't my client at the time."

You could see the wheels spinning in the sheriff's head. "What morning was that?"

"Thursday morning."

It must have hit the sheriff at the same time that it hit me because his eyes widened. The knife, Thursday morning, Duke's. It was Jeb. He must have picked up the knife after all the commotion. His memory must have come back. He had seen me as he was coming out of his haze. He figured it was my knife. It was the perfect opportunity to get even with Amber and me at the same time. He would kill her and frame me for the murder.

Eli watched the two of us for a moment, seemingly puzzled at our looks of realization. He broke the spell by continuing. "All of the evidence points to someone else killing Amber, staging it to look like a sexual assault, using my client's knife and leaving it at the scene to be easily found. Someone is trying to frame my client for her murder. My client has an alibi from two reliable witnesses and one of those witnesses can testify that he lost that knife three days ago."

The sheriff sat motionless. The detective was still fidgeting with his pen and looking down at his pad of notes.

Eli broke the silence. "Jim, are you going to call Charlie, or am I?"

The sheriff just snorted. "Call Charlie? Why would I do that?"

Eli closed his portfolio and looked up with a big grin. "To have the Commonwealth's Attorney drop the charges against my client."

The sheriff chuckled. "You can try all the legal smoke and mirrors you like. I'm not calling Charlie 'cause your boy's guilty." The detective continued to fidget with his pen, never looking up at the two men.

Eli folded his hands and smiled up at the sheriff, holding his gaze for quite a while. Like the ground trembling before a volcano blows, you could feel the sheriff's anger building. Eli finally spoke. "Well, suit yourself then. I'll give Charlie a call." He slipped the pen back into his pocket and picked up the portfolio. Looking up, he said, "I'm advising my client not to answer any more questions. This interrogation is over."

The sheriff erupted, "Any MORE questions? He hasn't answered ANY questions!"

Eli smiled calmly back. "I know." He continued to smile at the sheriff. He was enjoying this way too much.

The sheriff pointed at me and shouted to Cooper, "Get him out of here."

Eli and I left the room together, him to call the judge and me to sit in the holding cell. I couldn't see a clock, but it seemed that I waited quite a while.

Eventually, Cooper showed up at the cell door and announced, "You're free to go. The charges have been dropped."

As I stepped into the open office, I saw Eli standing off to the left, waiting for me. With a broad grin, he commented, "Come along, John Smith. We've got some talking to do." I smiled. It was all a joke now, but the John Smith thing wasn't going away.

Storms of the Past

Sitting in the car outside the sheriff's office, Eli slid the key into the ignition and then turned to me. "Well… Joe or Joseph?"

"Joe," I said quietly.

"Well, Joe, you just got some damn-fine, free legal services. You still think you're being underpaid for painting the house?" He grinned.

I couldn't help it. I laughed. It had been a tense few hours. I needed that release and Eli knew it. He chuckled along with me.

The remnants of a buttery sunset melted along the western horizon. To the east a faint sliver of moon hovered above the trees. We were in that gray, dusky limbo that is neither day nor night. Eli said he'd drive me home but wanted to stop at his place first. He still had a lot of questions. As we drove, something about Eli's unexpected rescue niggled in the corner of my mind. I had to ask, "How'd you know that I'd been arrested? I know it's a small town and news travels fast, but that was way too fast."

Eli smiled and shot me a glance before looking back at the road. "Molly came straight to me after the deputies carted you off. She asked me to help. Offered to pay. I told her there was no need. I'd do it for free."

He glanced over at me again. "She likes you, you know?"

I nodded. "I know, but trouble follows me everywhere. She seems like a really nice person. I don't think she needs the kind of storms that sweep through my life."

Eli nodded. "Maybe." Pointing out the window, he said, "See that field over there." Rows of corn stalks flickered by in the waning light. "Notice how yellow and stunted the stalks are? We haven't seen rain here in weeks. Without storms, things die. You need both storms and sunlight."

"Yeah, but my life seems to be constant storms. You know, too much rain… kills."

Eli glanced over with that signature wry smile. "Maybe you need a little sunlight to temper those storms."

I knew he was referring to Molly and gave him a wry smile of my own.

We drove the rest of the trip in silence.

Once in his house, Eli had me settle into one of the leather chairs across from his desk. I wasn't sure what else there was to talk about, but, as he pointed out, this was free legal service. I decided to humor him. Eli hung his suit coat on an old, wooden coat rack in the corner of the room, shuffled back to the desk, and settled into the comfortable chair behind it. After opening his leather portfolio, he folded his hands on top of it, and raised his gaze to meet mine. "Joe, I'm your attorney. Anything that you tell me is subject to attorney-client privilege. It stays between us. So, here's my question, and I'm going to be blunt. Did you kill her?"

My body shot up erect in the chair, no longer amused. "No, I didn't kill Amber. I thought you believed that!"

Eli never blinked, but held up his hand and in a quiet soothing tone he said, "No, no, no. You misunderstand."

Uneasily, I settled back into my chair.

"I meant did you kill your wife?" He was still calm and steady.

I wasn't. I jumped from my chair. "No need to drive me home. I'll walk." I stormed toward the door.

Again, came Eli's calm voice. "Now, now, Joe. I didn't mean to upset you. I just want to hear the story straight from you. No talk about evidence or witnesses. No talk about dropped charges. I just want to hear the simple truth."

For some reason, the tone of his voice had a calming effect. I stopped at the door and sighed letting my pent-up anger escape into the room. Quietly, I said, "No, I didn't kill Lauren. I loved her."

Eli's voice was steady and calm. "Good. That's all I needed to hear. I believe you. Please come back and have a seat."

I hesitated, looked down the hallway toward the front door, and then, glancing back at Eli, returned to my seat.

He looked me squarely in the eyes. "Joe, doesn't it strike you as odd that most people's scrape with the law is nothing more than a speeding ticket, yet in just a matter of months you've been wrongly accused of killing two women?"

I thought about it for a moment and responded, "Like I said, trouble seems to follow wherever I go."

Eli shook his head. "I'm not so sure it's that simple. Will you humor an old man? I don't have much to keep me occupied any more, and you've given me a great deal of entertainment today… at your expense, unfortunately." He winked at me and smiled. "Will you give me just a bit of time and tell me about what happened down in Fayetteville?"

I considered it. I was a very private person, but Eli had saved me. I felt I owed him something. I nodded. "I probably need to start a bit earlier because the trouble started before I got back to Fayetteville."

I went on to tell Eli the story of my deployment to Afghanistan and how things went south for me while I was there – the nightmares, the inability to sleep, the tremors, the outbursts, the inability to function. I was sent back home, diagnosed with PTSD, and eventually released on disability.

Eli listened intently, taking lengthy notes and occasionally asking questions about my unit, where we were deployed, and dates of events.

I looked up at the ceiling, my pain escaping in one slow breath. "It really started falling to pieces when I got back in the States. I was withdrawn and difficult to live with. I had trouble finding a job, and the few I did find, I couldn't keep. The job problems caused money problems and put a real strain on our marriage. I started drinking heavily which only made things worse. I loved my wife, but we argued a lot. She just wanted the old Joe back. *I* wanted the old Joe back. I knew he was locked away somewhere deep inside, but I just couldn't find the key."

Eli waited for me to continue, but I didn't. "So, tell me about what happened to your wife."

I looked back from the ceiling to Eli. "Well, where do I start? The night before the accident, Lauren mentioned that her car's check-engine light had come on. I suggested that we switch cars the next day, and I'd take her car to the shop. Later that night, I went to a local bar and, as usual, drank myself into a stupor. I'm not even sure how I got home. I woke up the next day with the police banging on the door to tell me that Lauren had been in a fatal car crash on her way to work." The last few words were more moaned than spoken.

I stopped for a moment, looked away, and tried to hide the tears that were coming. Swiping my fingers at the corners of my eyes, I took a deep breath. "A few days later, I was arrested. They said the brakes on the car had been tampered with, and they'd received a tip from a guy who spoke with me in the bar the night before. According to this guy, I said that I was fed up with my wife and I was going to kill her." Again, I stopped to swallow back the tears. "I know that I was a worthless shell of the man she married, but I still loved her. I would never have said that… drunk or sober."

Eli asked, "So why did they drop the charges?"

"According to the police, the guy who tipped them off disappeared. Actually, I don't think he ever existed. I think it was just a story they used to convince me to admit guilt, save myself from a worse fate."

Eli flashed a knowing smile. He'd probably seen the "make things easier on yourself" tactic before.

"Anyway, they didn't have enough evidence to make the charges stick and decided to drop them… wait for more evidence to surface… give them a better chance in court."

Eli nodded. "So, Lauren was driving your car on the day of the accident?"

I was looking down at the floor now, trying unsuccessfully to hide the tears that ran freely. I said quietly, "Yeah… it should have been me, not her."

Eli let me have my moment. Then he said, closing his portfolio, "Well you certainly have had your share of stormy weather, John Smith."

I managed a weak smile.

He asked if I'd like a drink before he drove me home. I passed on the offer. We drove to the cabin in silence.

In the Dark of Night

I was exhausted, more weary than sleepy. It looked like it might be another in a long string of sleepless nights. The cabin was cold from a day of constant air conditioning. I shut off the lights, turned off the sputtering machine for some quiet, and lay back on the bed listening to the muted sound of the frogs outside the cabin. Scenes from an earlier life floated in and out of my thoughts. Where did things go wrong? How did I end up broke and broken? It was hard to find the exact moment that everything fell apart.

At some point, the weight of a life in shambles brought down the darkness of sleep.

Somewhere in a haze, a sound. Eyelids strained to open against the weight of exhaustion. Only quiet darkness as they crept down again. A click. Another. My eyes were wide open now. What was that sound? The faint whine of a door hinge. The pale moonlight cast ghostly shadows on the walls. A sliver of light spread across the floor from the doorway, a distorted shadow was cast in the slice of moonlight. I tensed preparing for the moment that I'd need to recoil. The shadow moved, quietly nearing the bed. Against the moonlit backdrop outside the open door, I could make out a dark silhouette. As my eyes adjusted to the layers of darkness, the outline became clearer. It was a woman's figure. Was this a nightmare? Was this Amber's spirit come back to haunt me... or perhaps warn me? I sat up, throwing my legs over the edge of the bed to face her. "Who's there?"

There was a quiet, familiar giggle. "It's me." The voice was Molly's.

I felt the knots in my shoulders and back release as I exhaled, "I think you just took ten years off my life."

Again, she giggled as she drew closer. In the moonlight, I could make out the faint features of her face. She was even more beautiful than I remembered. She wore a short, loose-fitting dress, maybe a nightgown. It was hard to tell in the dark.

"How did you get in here? The door was locked."

I could make out a faint smirk as she shook her head. She held out her hand, palm open, the moonlight glinting from a key. "I lived here for most of my life. Do you really think I don't still have a key?"

I chuckled at my stupidity.

She began running her fingers through my long, wild hair. "We were at the best part of our day when everything went crazy," she sighed. "I've been lying in bed and sleep won't come. All that I can think about is that kiss. I came to see if you want to pick up where we left off."

I smiled up from the bed and hoped that she could see it in the moonlight. "I can't think of anything that I want more."

She leaned down and brushed her lips over mine, at first softly and tenderly and then with increasing passion. She straightened up and slipped the straps of her loose-fitting dress from her shoulders. It slid to the floor, landing with a soft flutter at her feet. Next, she reached up with both hands and unpinned her hair. With a toss of her head, it came tumbling down, cascading over her bare shoulders and breasts. She was shapely and exciting. She straddled my legs and pushed me back on the bed as she fell into my arms. We kissed with feverish intensity as I caressed her smooth skin. I could still smell the faint scent of gardenias. Her hair flowed in waves framing her face as she looked down on me.

Suddenly, she jerked back, screaming. She seemed suspended above me, her hands grasping desperately at her hair.

Then I saw it, a second figure silhouetted in the dark, a large figure. It was Jeb, Molly's hair gripped firmly in his left hand, suspending her upper body above the bed. He yanked causing her back to arch at a painful angle making it difficult for her to get her feet on the floor. Before I could react, his right hand appeared at her throat. The glint of a long blade was unmistakable. This was no pocketknife. Even in the dark, I could tell it was a fixed blade, probably one used for field dressing game, very sharp and nasty. Jeb held the blade to Molly's throat. The weight of her lower body pinned my hips to the bed. If I tried throwing her off, she could be sliced accidentally or purposely. I felt helpless.

She let out a shrill cry, trying frantically to free herself. Jeb snatched her hair tighter, twisting his fingers in the strands. "You whore!" he growled. "Cheating on me with this worthless wife killer! You're both gonna' pay."

Molly sobbed, pleading, "Jeb, please let go. Please. Please, Jeb."

He tightened his grip again and shouted down at me. "Hey, boy. Want to watch as I slice her up?" He raised the blade and flattened it against her face with the point near the corner of her eye. He slowly slid the flat of the blade down her face. Near her chin, he turned the blade so that it nicked her, sending a small stream of blood running down her neck. He continued the track of the blade down her breasts again nicking her twice. The cuts were small, but the streams of blood made a ghastly scene.

I didn't see a good ending. Jeb wasn't going to let us go. He was going to kill us both. I had to chance it. I had to take the knife from him. I waited until his hand was within range of my left hand and farther from her throat. Attacking with both hands, I twisted my body so that I could get my right hand close enough. I slid my left hand between his arm and her body, pulling outward to move the knife away from her. At the same time, I grabbed his fingers wrapped around the knife with my right hand twisting the blade away from her. I was counting on Jeb letting go of Molly's hair to use his free hand to gain control of the knife. As I grabbed for his hand, my fingers, wet with perspiration, slipped, and his knife hand came free. Before I could grab again, he recovered, yanked her head up higher. As she screamed and flailed, he slashed the blade across her throat, bathing us in a torrent of blood.

A Plan

I awoke screaming, shuddering, crying. Of all the horrible nightmares over the years, this was the worst. They all had dark figures and unspeakable acts, but they were always directed at me. This was the first one that I could remember where I was a spectator in another person's terror and death. The most frightening part was that, in the darkest recesses of my mind, there was Si. His wicked grin revealing that he knew what I was just realizing, Molly had become much too important to me. This nightmare rocked me. There'd be no more sleep tonight. I turned the lights on and sat down with a cold beer, trying to calm myself. I was unnerved, and it took quite a while to regain my composure.

The nightmare and the certainty that Jeb now knew that I was the one who blindsided him, made it clear that it was time for me to try to cobble the pile of junk from Eli's into some type of defense system. His next drunken spell was sure to bring revenge. My first plan was to fix the broken arm on the security light and install it outside the cabin. As I thought through the plan, it made less and less sense. The whole idea behind a security light is to frighten off intruders by making them visible to others. The cabin was in the middle of a wooded lot. Would anyone really care if a light came on? The Grovers were the only ones out there, and they were quiet neighbors who were good at keeping secrets.

What I needed was a way to know if someone approached the cabin. I wrestled with the problem for a while and finally came up with a plan that I wasn't sure would work. It would require a long run of extension cords. I wasn't an electrician, but I knew that the longer the run, the greater the possibility for loss in voltage. Luckily, Eli's extension cords were heavy duty, but this would be tricky. I would need some daylight to test my plan. It was still dark outside, so I started with the other piece of the plan, covering the windows. Using duct tape, I covered the inside of each window with the cardboard from Eli's. I used the tape to seal around the edges and to seal up where I joined pieces. I double-checked to be sure that I could still unlock, open and close the windows. Now, peering eyes wouldn't be able to see in.

I looked out the door. The first light of day was rising like a mist through the trees. It was just bright enough to see. The lane leading into the clearing was shaped somewhat like a question mark. Although it opened to the left front of the cabin, it actually curved around the side before winding down toward the highway. There wasn't a lot of distance between the lane and the left wall of the cabin, but the thick trees and underbrush made it impossible to see the building until you emerged into the clearing.

A couple of the extension cords appeared to be 100 feet in length. I ran one out of the left window of the cabin and fought my way through the underbrush toward the lane. I reached the end of the extension cord as I waded out of the trees. So, the distance was OK.

Now, I would see if the electrical piece of the plan would work. I cut the female end off the extension cord and spliced the wires into the wires of the motion sensor using electrician's tape to secure the connections. Next, I removed the metal arm with the light, cutting the wires. I took the second extension cord and cut off both ends. Splicing the cord into the light allowed me to have a 100-foot separation between the motion sensor and the light it controlled. I used the duct tape to secure the sensor to a tree facing the lane. Ready for a test, I jogged back to the cabin and plugged the extension cord into an outlet. I then returned to the sensor on the lane. After adjusting the sensor's settings, I placed it in test mode. Amazingly, when I moved near the sensor, the light came on. Satisfied with my MacGyver contraption, I ran the second cord with the spliced light fixture back through the underbrush and into the window of the cabin. Using the duct tape again, I attached the broken metal arm to the wall and angled the light toward the bed. Now, if someone came down the lane at night, it would trigger the sensor on the lane and turn on the light inside the cabin, waking me up. The cardboard in the windows would prevent the light from being seen outside.

Test mode appeared to give me about fifteen seconds of light. I walked the distance between the sensor and the front door several times. It took about thirty seconds to walk from the sensor and reach the front door. My plan was to leave the sensor on test mode. I just wanted enough light to wake me up. Once awake, I would slip out the back window of the cabin into the trees. The light would go out and Jeb would find a dark, empty cabin. I wasn't yet sure what would happen after that. It was still a plan in progress, but at least I now had a way of being alerted if he came to pay a visit.

Conversations

I thought about going to Duke's for breakfast but figured that Molly knew more about me now than she'd ever wanted to know. She'd probably be glad if she never saw me again. Instead, I scrambled a couple of eggs and heated up some vile tasting two-day-old coffee.

The sun was still low when I locked up and walked off toward Eli's. As I moved down the lane, I continued my new routine of sweeping away all footprints and tire tracks behind me. This procedure made moving down the lane a slow process, but I had all the time in the world. This morning was particularly slow due to all the cruiser tracks from the day before. But as Eli had asked the first time we spoke, "You don't have anything better to do, do you?" The answer was still the same—I didn't.

Arriving at Eli's, I prepared to complete the front of the house. I still had a bit of exterior white to apply and two shutters to paint. My plan was to finish the painting and hang the shutters before the end of the day. With the front finished, I could have some sense of completion. Although I had promised Eli that I would finish the job, I had an uneasy feeling that I should run, but I needed money. Maybe he would pay me if the street side of the house was completed. Run? And leave Molly behind? Probably the best thing for her, but the idea gnawed at me the rest of the day.

I went straight to the shed and laid out the remaining shutters, opened the black paint, and began applying it with steady brush strokes. I heard the back screen door slam and glanced up to find Eli shuffling toward me in the same pajama shorts and T-shirt I had seen before.

He stopped short and watched me for a moment. "You look like Satan lashed you to the back of a pickup truck and dragged you through a field."

I'd never heard it put quite that way before, but I caught the image. Stress and a string of sleepless nights had me looking ragged. I had seen it in the mirror earlier that morning.

He followed with, "How are you doing?"

"I'll make it."

He looked skeptical. "Seems to me you should be resting today, not working."

"I don't know what rest is anymore. I'd rather stay busy." I gave a weak smile. "Keeps the mind occupied."

Eli nodded, his expression reflecting a sad understanding. "I'll bring you something cold to drink in a bit." He made his way back to the house, disappearing inside.

I finished up the shutters and left them to dry as I dragged the heavy extension ladder back to the front of the house along with white paint and a drop cloth. I hadn't been up on the ladder very long before Eli appeared on the front porch, dressed in khakis and a dress shirt open at the collar. He carried two cold bottles of beer and invited me down to join him. We sat in the wicker chairs, enjoying the cold liquid in the clammy, humid air. As we sat drinking, Eli asked, "Have you paid attention to the news much over the past year?"

I laughed, "The other day, you gave me a hard time because I wasn't sure what month it was. I can't believe you asked that question."

Eli smirked. "So, I'll take that as a 'no.'"

I nodded. I wasn't sure where he was going with this, but he didn't say any more. His bottle empty, Eli stood and stepped back to admire the house.

"It's looking good. I think I'll go inside and let you finish." Then, off he shuffled.

Eli appeared again around lunchtime with sandwiches and cold iced tea and one more time in the afternoon as I was hanging the shutters. This time, he brought ice-cold beer. Handing me the bottle as I stepped off the ladder, he said, "Let me know when you're finished. I have something I think will interest you."

It all seemed a bit cryptic, but Eli liked being mysterious. He was a nice guy, but he was a bit controlling. Nodding, I lifted the bottle to my lips as I looked back to admire the almost complete front portion of the house.

About half an hour later, I dragged the ladder, paint, and drop cloth back to the shed. I cleaned out the brushes and put everything back in its place.

As I arrived at the front porch, I found Eli surveying my work. He nodded his head with a satisfied smile. "You do good work, John Smith." He shot me a big grin. I grinned back.

Eli looked off at clouds building along the western horizon and commented, "I hear we're in for thunderstorms tonight." He continued to stare in the direction of the flickering sky and listened to the faint rumble of thunder. "Yes, sir," he muttered. "Fire from heaven."

Shifting his gaze back to me, he opened the door and waved, "Come on inside, I've got a few things to show you."

I followed Eli into the office where we sat just a few hours earlier. He motioned me to one of the chairs as he moved behind the desk to take a seat. Sliding open a desk drawer, he removed a manila folder, and placed it on the desk in front of him.

"Early this morning, I contacted an old associate of mine up in Fairfax. Back in the day, he provided investigative services for me. I shared some of the information from our meeting last night and asked him to do some checking to see if he could dig up anything interesting related to your wife's death. He didn't find anything directly related, but he did find some very interesting coincidences. He sent me links to several articles he found. I've printed them."

Opening the folder, he lifted the top sheet. As he slid it across the desk to me, he explained, "I asked earlier if you paid attention to the news. I wasn't sure if you'd seen this."

The sheet was a printout of the Washington Post website. The headline read, "Congress Investigates Military Abuse."

Eli asked me to note the date. At first, I held the paper in my hands, but as I read, my fingers began to tremble. The tremors came on so strong that it made reading the jumping text impossible. I placed the paper on the desktop and dragged my chair closer so that I could see it clearly. The article outlined investigations into accusations of atrocities committed by a small group of individuals in Afghanistan. The unit under investigation was mine. Once I finished reading, I looked up at Eli.

"Notice the date of the news article? About the same time as your arrest in North Carolina."

I was trying to calm my hands with little success. I didn't see the connection and must have looked puzzled because Eli lifted the second sheet from the folder and slid it across to me. It was the printout of an obituary.

"Do you know this guy?"

I nodded, "I knew him well. He was in my unit." I read over the obituary of Daniel Dryer. In the picture, he seemed younger and happier than I remembered him. I looked up at Eli.

"My associate tells me that Mr. Dryer hung himself. Note the date of the obituary."

The cause of death didn't surprise me. What happened over there could twist you up inside. What did surprise me was the date of the obituary. It was about the same time as the Washington Post article.

Before I had much time to think about it, Eli slid another sheet across to me. It was an obituary of another guy I knew, Ben Faust. Like Dan, he had been a member of my unit. Without being asked, I looked at the date. Again, it was near the time of the Washington Post article. I gave Eli a surprised look.

"My associate tells me that Mr. Faust swallowed a bottle full of sleeping pills one night and never woke up."

Eli then slid the printout of a news article across the desk. Without being asked, I checked the date. It was just a few days following the obituaries. The headline announced, "Two Killed by Friendly Fire." I hated the term. There was nothing "friendly" about being in the line of fire, regardless of the source. I scanned the article to find the names, Corporal Marty Levinson and Sergeant Simon 'Si' Willis. I thought how ironic. I closed my eyes and could still hear Si's threatening voice after the first "conversation" he and I ever had.

*   *   *

"Look, new boy, the battlefield's a dangerous place. Accidents?" Si made a sweeping gesture with his hands. "Well... they happen." He gave a twisted grin. "I wouldn't want one to happen to you." He took me firmly by the arm. "That's why we need to have each other's backs... if you get my drift." I may not have been the brightest guy in the world, but I knew a threat when I heard it. I got his drift.

*   *   *

"Joe... Joe?" Eli's voice jerked me back into the present. "Do you see any connection between these men and yourself?"

I nodded slowly, looking down at the papers spread before me on the desk. "During my tour in Afghanistan, the five of us were sometimes involved in special missions."

Eli looked questioningly at me. "What kind of 'special' missions?"

I didn't hear him at first. I was replaying the nightmares in my head. The tremors were now so bad that I shivered as if immersed in frigid water.

"Joe, what kind of 'special' missions?"

I kept my eyes focused on the desk ashamed to make eye contact with Eli. "Si called them 'conversations.' He would occasionally come to us and say that we needed to have a 'conversation' with some tribal leader to help them cooperate in some way."

Eli waited for more, but I was silent. He prodded, "Well, that doesn't sound so bad."

"You don't get it," I continued to speak to the desk. "Si liked to say that we were helping these men appreciate their families. He said it was like a public service." I gave a faint, half-hearted chuckle.

Eli wouldn't let it go. "And just how did you 'help' them appreciate their family?"

I closed my eyes and there was Si, his crooked smile and his dark eyes.

*   *   *

"See, new boy, a man's most vulnerable pressure point is right here." He thumped the center of his chest with two fingers. *"Find out who he loves and then apply pressure. He will learn to appreciate what he has."* There was an evil glint in his soulless eyes. *"Sometimes it's his wife, or a teenage daughter."* The corners of his mouth rose slightly in a cold smile, tantalized by the thought. *"Maybe it's a toddler or a newborn. Whatever works."* He motioned with the palm of his hand as if this were a simple equation. *"He decides how long the conversation lasts."* But with Si, it always lasted longer than the man chose. Si called it insurance. We couldn't make it too easy for the guy. Had to be sure that he didn't forget. I was certain it was just pure, sick pleasure.

*   *   *

"Joe... Joe?" Again, it was Eli's voice.

I opened my eyes grateful to leave Si behind.

"How did you help them appreciate their family?"

I let out years of pain in one long breath. Looking down, I wrung my trembling hands, much in the way you would scrub away dirt or blood. "We were sent to do things... things that I'm sure weren't sanctioned by the Pentagon. Things that haunt me in my nightmares.

Horrible things." At this point, I became aware that I was rocking back and forth in the chair like a child.

Eli sat in the heavy silence, watching, waiting.

"That's why things went bad for me." I continued rocking, streams cascading over the dams that I had built. "I just let it happen. I… I did nothing to stop it… nothing." After a painful pause, I spoke again to the floor. "I couldn't live with myself. I couldn't eat. I couldn't sleep. I was worthless… and dangerous. They sent me home."

After another heavy silence, Eli spoke up. "Joe?"

I looked up through tear-filled eyes.

"Were there any others involved in these 'special' missions?"

I shook my head. "No, just the five of us. Si jokingly called us *The Brotherhood*. We knew we were out-of-bounds."

Eli sat for a moment. I glanced up to see him, furrowed brow, narrowed eyes, like a chess player studying the board, looking for the pattern of moves and counter moves about to unfold.

"Who ordered these 'conversations'?"

I shrugged, looking again at my hands, still trying to wipe away the stains. "Si never said."

Eli paused for a moment and then continued. "You told me your wife was driving your car the day of the accident. I don't think it was an accident at all. Someone tampered with the brakes, expecting you to be at the wheel. Someone was trying to eliminate all the witnesses to what happened in Afghanistan. They managed to kill the other four men in your unit and made it look like suicide or an accident. For example, a car accident."

Eli waited for that idea to sink in before he started up again. "I have a second theory. They weren't counting on your wife driving your car that morning. When the accident killed the wrong person, they tried to frame you for the murder. A convicted murderer doesn't make much of a witness before a Congressional committee. And no one questions an inmate being killed in prison. You know, violent population and all." He continued, "Actually, you probably wouldn't have survived a week in prison."

I was confused and was having trouble wrapping my brain around all of this. His theory was just too cloak and dagger for a small town nobody like me. "I don't know… I just don't know." After all these months of believing that the police had tried to set me up so that I'd confess, it was hard to switch gears.

"Joe, what happened after the charges were dropped in Fayetteville?"

My hands had settled some at this point. I ran my trembling fingers through my hair sweeping it backward as I exhaled. "Well, everything had fallen apart at that point. Our rocky financial situation had grown worse. My car was totaled, and my wife's car had been repossessed. Friends and relatives turned their backs on me. As soon as I was released, I went to our little townhouse and threw everything I owned in a backpack and a messenger bag. I stopped at an ATM and withdrew all the money I could and caught the first bus out of town. The destination didn't matter. I just wanted out. I've been floating from here to there ever since."

Eli sat, his elbows on the desk, fingertips together touching his lips. He separated his hands, swept up the papers, and placed them in the folder in front of him. "It sounds as if you just dropped off the face of the earth, and they lost track of you. You may want to stay lost, but this recent arrest won't help."

I was struggling with Eli's theory. Dead? They were all dead? My wife? And then there was Jeb. I wasn't sure what to believe. My stomach churned from this nightmare of a roller coaster ride, and I feared the next twisting drop.

Song of Life and Death

As I walked the highway from Eli's, there was an eeriness to the late daylight. Dark clouds were building to the west and the sun setting behind them painted the edges of the ominous, black clouds with a counterpoint of brilliant white. I walked on in this strange twilight.

At the lane, I paid close attention to the dusty sections. Nothing. I continued to check along the entire length. There were no signs of foot or car traffic. As I passed the sensor tucked back in the trees, I wondered if the light had come on in the cabin. I decided to test it. I unlocked the cabin door and left it open so that I would be able to see inside. Walking back past the sensor, I turned and headed toward the cabin. A few seconds later as I rounded the trees into the clearing, I could see the lighted doorway. As I drew nearer, the light went out. It worked. This little test brought some small sense of relief.

Night was stealing through the trees quickly, and I could hear the growing rumble of thunder in the distance. There was something fascinating and beautiful about lightning. I dragged one of the chairs out into the clearing to watch the approaching light show accompanied by the orchestra of frogs. The storm was still distant. The trees blocked my view, but there were occasional flickers against the clouds above. As the light and sound moved to the north, it looked like the storm might miss us, but I could see more lightning to the west as well. As the mosquitoes joined the party, I decided to call it a night.

The long stretch of sleepless nights was catching up with me, and exhaustion weighed heavily on my eyelids. Locking the door, I propped the chair below the doorknob and switched off the lights. The frogs sang of love and hate… life and death. I fell asleep.

Stormy Night

Boom... crackle... sizzle... lightning strike... somewhere near. I was jolted from sleep... and the lightning was blinding! Lightning? Something wasn't right! The lightning didn't flicker. Why didn't it flicker? Not lightning. It was a bright light. THE LIGHT! It was the security light! Had to hurry! Made the window. Slipped the lock. Slid out as quietly as I could. I should've practiced this part. I fell out awkwardly. The light went dark as I slid the window closed. Not much time. I found the trail behind the cabin and followed it for a few feet. Then I left the path circling around, struggling through the underbrush to get a view of the front of the cabin. Had to be slow. Had to be quiet. Thunder crashed and boomed ever closer. The sky was a mixing bowl of light and darkness. To the east, the crescent moon could be seen just above the tree line. To the north and west, black clouds heaved like a living, breathing thing. The lightning was an uncertain strobe against the low hung clouds.

I'd managed to work my way to a point where I could see the front and the side of the cabin. A dark figure moved slowly toward the door. I couldn't make out any detail and the lightning wasn't cooperating. At the door, the figure stooped near the lock. Seconds later, the shadow stood and pushed against the door. I must not have wedged the chair solidly because I heard it clatter to the floor. Next, the shadow was swallowed by the blackness of the cabin doorway.

I continued moving slowly toward the front of the cabin until I was behind the Grovers, giving me a clear view of the door. There was still no visible movement.

Suddenly, light filled the cabin and spilled out the doorway into the clearing. The figure stood silhouetted in the backlight of the doorway. The intruder seemed to be as startled by the light as I was. The shadow spun around to face the inside of the cabin, looked quickly left and right, spun back again to look out the doorway. I couldn't grasp what was happening until I heard a series of pops coming from my right near the top of the lane. The pops were accompanied by flashes of light, but not lightning. There was the sound of splintering wood. I looked back to the cabin and the shadow in the doorway had slumped to the ground. The pops continued, giving way to a series of clicks, no flashes.

I was consumed by shock and confusion. A second person must have triggered the motion sensor, bringing on the cabin light. For some reason, the second figure emptied his gun into the silhouette in the doorway. The clicking sounds came as he continued to pull the trigger with an empty magazine.

I tried to focus on this second figure, but his form blended into the dark trees near the end of the lane. As the shadowy figure cleared the trees. A bright flash of lightning lit up the clearing. The shadowy monster had a face. It was Jeb dressed in camo shirt and pants. But if that was Jeb, who was the other shadow? I glanced back at the cabin where the shadowy figure lay prone on the ground. The moon cleared the clouds for just a moment as Jeb moved through the clearing. I could barely make him out. He raised a can to his lips, drank the last of its contents, and tossed it to the side. He appeared to stagger as he approached the motionless figure. I was so confused. This must be another nightmare. Who was the other figure?

Jamming his pistol in the waistband behind his back, Jeb leaned down and with both hands rolled the body over. He stood, a bit unsteady. Then he bent over, hands on knees to study the body. Having trouble seeing clearly in the dark, he knelt and brought his face closer to the face of the dark figure. His head shot backward. "Oh, Shit!" He brought his head down close again. "Shit! Shit! Shit!" His head came up again and swung from side to side as if he were looking for something. He stood up, turning slowly around searching the darkness. He left the body and wobbled through the cabin door, disappearing inside. The cursing became louder. He stepped out of the blackness of the cabin, still scanning the clearing and surrounding trees.

Jeb stepped out of the doorway and stood looking first at the body, then the trees, then the cabin, and again back to the body. He seemed to be unsure of what to do next. Eventually, he grabbed the arms of the dark figure and began dragging the lifeless shadow toward where I was hidden. I crouched in panic, hoping not to be seen. Just then, the skies opened, and large drops of rain came splattering down in a roar of water pelting the leaves and the ground. A curtain of water streamed down, obscuring my view. The dirt quickly turned to mud and everything became slippery from the rivers of rain.

Jeb struggled as he strained backward, yoked with the dead, dark weight. His already unsteady footing worsened as his feet slid and slipped in the mud. When he reached the underbrush, he struggled to push his back into the tangle of small limbs and vines. He strained against the underbrush only feet from where I crouched in the darkness. At one point, he twisted and heaved to break through the thicket. Cursing, he wrestled to free himself from some thorny vines. As he did, the gun in his waistband pulled free and fell next to his feet. In the struggle and the torrent of rain, he didn't notice. The rain continued to hammer everything below. Jeb pressed on, determined to hide the body deeper in the woods. A string of profanity continued as he fought his way through the tangle of foliage.

Soon, Jeb, angry and drunk, came crashing back into the clearing. He looked around, turning slowly one more time, muttering, "Where is that murdering bastard?"

How drunk was he? He killed Amber, not me. Peering into the rain-smeared darkness and finding nothing, he stumbled toward the lane, disappearing into the downpour. Seconds later, the light flashed on in the cabin as he passed the motion sensor. Fifteen seconds later, it was dark again.

The rain gave way to drizzle, and then the storm clouds gave way to moon and stars. I waited for a long time, uncertain of Jeb's return. When I finally thought it was safe, I stood and followed the trail of mangled foliage to the place where Jeb dragged the body. I had to know what just happened. Looking down on the pale face in the moonlight, none of it made sense. Somewhere in the back of my mind, the face seemed familiar. But who? Who was this man? Then it struck me. It was polo shirt. The guy who'd studied me so intently my first morning in the diner... and at LakeFest... but what brought him here?

Jeb must have riffled through his wallet trying to figure out the same thing. The wallet lay open in the weeds next to the body. I knelt and strained to read the driver's license. I didn't recognize the name, but the North Carolina license listed a Fayetteville address.

A chill swept over me like falling through ice into frigid water. Eli was right. That's why Jeb called me a murderer. He didn't frame me for Amber's murder. Her killer was lying at my feet. Polo shirt must have followed me into the diner that morning and in the clamor that followed, he picked up the knife unseen. When his attempt to frame me for Amber's murder failed, he came here to implement the ultimate solution. The irony of it all was that Jeb showed up to avenge Amber's death and unwittingly killed the real murderer.

Jeb was dangerous, unpredictable, and hated me. It wasn't safe for me to stay, but if I ran, what danger would I leave in my wake for Molly and Eli? Anyone who'd befriended me would be a target for Jeb's wrath. I wasn't sure who sent the dead assassin lying at my feet, but I was certain they would send others. I needed a plan that would allow me time to run, time to put distance between me and Bethany Crossing. Between Jeb and my unknown pursuers, I didn't have very good odds. My mind raced to find a solution. Jeb would sober up and realize that his gun was missing. He would be back… soon. I had to work quickly.

I rushed through the underbrush toward the cabin. Inside, I took down the shower curtain, emptied and grabbed my messenger bag, and returned to the body. On the way, I noticed a beer can near the cabin. It wasn't mine. That must have been what Jeb had thrown on the ground. I found a small stick and, running it into the open can, picked it up without touching it. There was a good chance that the can had Jeb's fingerprints on it, and I didn't want mine there as well. I placed the can in the messenger bag and continued on with the shower curtain. On the way, I did the same with Jeb's gun. I needed to move the body but without creating the trail of mangled underbrush that Jeb had left. I spread the shower curtain out next to the body and rolled him onto it. I took off my shirt and, using it to cover my hand, I picked up the wallet and dropped it into the messenger bag with the beer can and the gun. Wrapping the curtain around the body, I hefted it up. It was a struggle to get the body over my shoulder, but I finally managed. Now, was the tricky part. I needed to hide the body. I had to locate Molly's "castle" in the dark. The crescent moon now peered out between dark clouds. It shed enough light for me to find my way through the darkness. I got my bearings and headed off in what I thought was the right direction. I was off, but not by much. I eventually saw the oak tree to my left. Dragging the body off the curtain and into the "castle" was a bit of a challenge, but after cursing and sweating, I had the body hidden.

Now, I was scrambling to finish. Using my T-shirt as a glove, I removed the items from the messenger bag and left them sitting next to the body. I worked my way back to the cabin with the shower curtain, only getting off track a bit. I rinsed the curtain in the shower until it was free of blood and dirt. I rehung it.

Throwing everything that I owned in my backpack and the messenger bag, I headed out the door. My foot hit something as I stepped away from the door. It was a pistol partially covered with mud. I'd already hidden Jeb's gun, so this must have been in polo shirt's hands when he was shot. I picked it up, wiped it off, and threw it in the messenger bag. If people were out to get me, it could come in handy.

I hurried down the lane in the dark for the last time. As I stepped out onto the highway, there was quite a scene farther up the road. Two cars were stopped on an angle by the side of the road, their headlights aimed toward a silver and black pickup truck that was nose down in the ditch next to the road. The rear of the truck sat up at an awkward angle, only one rear wheel touched the ground. Several people scurried around near the cab of the truck and from the excited tone of their voices, I could tell that someone was inside. Sirens wailed off in the distance. Turning away, I walked the opposite direction toward town.

The Letter

At Eli's house, I pounded on the door without an answer. I hammered a second time, longer and louder. A rectangle of light streaming from an upstairs window splashed across the front lawn. I pounded again, long and hard.

Lights came on downstairs. Eventually, Eli opened the front door. He was half-asleep. The other half was angry.

"Do you know what time it is?" he barked.

Glancing around furtively into the darkness, I begged, "Eli, can I come in? I need your help."

I must have looked like one of my nightmares, rain-soaked and frantic. Eli caught the urgency in my voice and searched the darkness as if he sensed imminent danger.

He ushered me through the door and into his office, locking the front door behind him.

"What's going on, Joe? What's got you so spooked?" He motioned to the chair, but I shook my head. I couldn't sit. The adrenaline was still running crazy. I needed to get out of town.

"Eli, you were right! I was stupid, but you nailed it. They're after me."

"Who's after you?"

"I don't know who. The same people responsible for those obituaries you showed me. They sent someone to kill me tonight. I'll tell you everything, but first I need to use your computer. Do you have envelopes and stamps?"

Eli looked puzzled as he motioned to the chair behind the desk. "Sure, I have both."

I sat at the computer. It was a dinosaur from the ice age of technology. As I waited for the old machine to boot up, I noticed a mahogany framed 8x10 photo sitting next to it on the desk. The big monitor had blocked my view of it from the other side of the desk. It had obviously been taken at a professional photography studio. It was the picture of a happy, smiling family. There was a much younger Eli in a dark suit, white shirt, and red tie. Seated next to him was a beautiful, slender woman in a perfectly tailored red dress. Unsuccessfully posed between them was a little girl in a flouncy, besparkled red dress with a mischievous twinkle in her eyes. This was a new revelation. Eli had a daughter.

My attention shifted as the desktop icons flashed up on the screen. I opened the word processing software and typed two brief letters. I printed two copies of the first letter and one copy of the second. Eli produced three envelopes and three stamps from a desk drawer. After a couple of quick web searches, I had the addresses I needed. I sealed up the three letters addressed them, stamped them, and said, "OK, I've got one last favor to ask."

Eli, the person always in control, looked uneasy with the unknown request but asked what he could do to help.

"I need you to drive me to the nearest bus station. I've got to get out of here, now." The bus station was miles away in a neighboring town along the interstate.

"Joe, maybe you're overreacting."

I shook my head, "Two people tried to kill me tonight. I'm lucky to be alive, but luck only lasts so long. Let's go. I'll tell you the story in the car."

Eli stood silent for a moment, his eyes wide. "Let me slip some 'outside' clothes on." He disappeared but was back in a few minutes dressed and ready to leave. As we stepped out the back door headed toward the Lincoln, we both searched the darkness for shadows.

The headlights cut through the darkness as I began my story. By the time we reached my lane, I'd told him about my makeshift early warning system, the dark figure in the doorway, Jeb's violent arrival, and his attempt to hide the body.

By this time, the accident just up the road was clearing. A sheriff's cruiser was pulling away and a paramedic was closing the back doors of an empty ambulance. A wrecker was attempting to remove the truck from the ditch as several people stood by watching.

Eli whistled, "Jeb really did a number on his truck!"

"That's Jeb's truck?"

Eli nodded.

"Slow down," I almost shouted.

Eli let up on the accelerator of the old Lincoln. As we approached, I could see Jeb among the bystanders. As we crawled past the accident, I told Eli to stop.

"Stop? What for?" Eli shot me a hard look.

"Just do it. I want to talk to Jeb."

"Are you crazy? He tried to kill you!"

"Just stop!"

Eli pulled up by the side of the road. I opened the door and stood silhouetted in the light, looking toward the truck. Seconds later, Jeb looked up. I motioned to him. I could tell as he leaned toward me, shielding his eyes from the wrecker's lights, that he was having trouble telling who was waving to him. He walked toward me, his gait a bit unsteady. At some point, recognition set in because his fists clenched, and his pace quickened.

As he drew close, I said, "I guess it's your night for accidents."

He glowered at me. He had a nasty, swollen red lump on his forehead, probably from the impact of the crash. Glancing at Eli in the car and back at the people near the wrecker, he must have reconsidered his impulse to hit me. I started up quickly before he changed his mind.

"I want to tell you a story. I think you'll like it."

He spat out, "I don't have time for this," and turned to walk away.

I raised my voice slightly. "It's about a drunken deputy who went into the woods one night looking for revenge."

He spun back around. His eyes narrowed.

I lowered my voice to be sure that only Eli and Jeb could hear the rest. "Yep, this deputy killed a man in cold blood, but it was the wrong person."

Jeb's eyes widened.

"So, he dragged the body off into the woods to hide it."

Jeb snorted, "No one would believe that fairy tale."

I held up my hand. "Wait, I haven't gotten to the best part. What the deputy didn't know was that the man he intended to kill saw the whole thing. After the deputy left, this guy moved the body and hid it in a new place. Another thing the deputy didn't realize was that he dropped his gun."

At this point, Jeb reached behind his back. Finding nothing, he then looked toward the truck as if willing the gun to be there.

As I began again, he turned back, his eyes wide. "Yep, he left behind his gun, an empty beer can, and the dead man's wallet, all with his fingerprints on them, all of them now hidden with the body."

I paused to let this sink in. "But that's not all. The guy who hid the evidence wrote letters to the Virginia State Police giving the details of this cold-blooded murder and giving them directions on how to find the evidence."

Jeb's eyes grew even bigger.

I continued, "The guy gave the letters to his friends and told them that if the deputy ever hurt either of them, the letters were to go in the mail. It would be the last time he would hurt anyone."

Jeb's lips moved, but it took a few seconds before he could get the words out. He stammered, "The dead man had a gun. The deputy would claim self-defense." He was trying to recover. His smile was half-hearted, unsure.

I shook my head. "Ah, but *I'm* writing this story and in my story, there is no second gun. The only gun the state police find is the deputy's." Then, with a grin I added, "And the icing on the cake is that the deputy runs his truck off the road near the scene of the murder, placing him there at the time of death."

My expression turned dark, my voice deliberate. "If you put your hands on Molly or Eli, if you even look at them the wrong way, that letter goes in the mail. The deputy in my story goes to prison for murder. I hear very unpleasant things happen to deputies who end up in prison. You don't want to be that guy." I paused for emphasis and then slid into the open door of the Lincoln, closed the door, and said to Eli, "Let's get out of here."

As we pulled off, I looked in the sideview mirror. Jeb stood motionless watching the taillights disappear in the darkness. Eli looked over at me with the broadest smile I'd ever seen on his face.

Unforgiven Sins

We drove in silence. I was still trying to make sense of everything that had happened in the past few hours. Finally, I broke the quiet spell. "I noticed the photo on your desk. I didn't know that you had a daughter."

Eli gave me a sideways glance. "You never asked." He sighed. "She's grown now, married with a little girl of her own."

"Really?"

Eli nodded.

"Well, what do you know? Eli's a grandpa." The pained expression on his face told me that I'd hit a raw nerve. "Where do they live?"

"Here in Bethany Crossing." His voice was flat, not the tone of a doting grandparent.

I knew the answer to the next question before I even asked it. "How long has it been since you've seen them?"

"Seen them?" He paused. "I see them every Sunday in church. I sit on the back pew and watch them from a distance. My daughter hasn't spoken to me in years." He pursed his lips for just a moment. "I've never held my granddaughter." His voice was tired and his eyes glistened.

"Eli, that family in that photo on your desk looks happy. What happened?"

He surprised me by asking, "Joe, how do you measure success?"

"Success?" I struggled for an answer. "Money, I guess… or maybe power… and then there's fame."

"Ah," he exhaled, letting his exclamation hang in the air. "The three weird sisters."

"The what?"

He glanced from the road with a faint smile.

"The three witches in Shakespeare's *Macbeth*."

He glanced again. I was still lost.

"In Shakespeare's play, the main character, Macbeth, meets three witches, the weird sisters, as he returns from battle. They foretell of his rise to the throne. What better success, right? But what their incantations fail to reveal are the costs of becoming king. They fail to tell him that it will cost his reputation, his peace of mind, and eventually his life."

Eli glanced at me again, "You see, Joe, money, power, and fame are the modern-day weird sisters, divining success, but they obscure the dreadful price in the mist of their dark deception. I was a gullible, small-town boy who listened as they hissed their gilded prophecies, never thinking that someday the bill would come due. But come due, it did. The real measure of success is the cost… the price you pay. In my case, I can measure my success in deceitful dealings, broken promises, broken hearts… and ultimately a shattered family."

I watched the white lines of the highway flashing by in the windshield with Eli's reflected face superimposed on the glass. He appeared to be in a trance, maybe gazing into the crystal ball as the dark shadows of what could have been danced to the chanting of the three weird sisters.

The spell was broken as he recited, more to the universe than to me, "If I have the gift of prophecy and can fathom all mysteries and all knowledge, and if I have a faith that can move mountains, but do not have love, I am nothing."

It sounded familiar, but I couldn't place it. "Shakespeare?" I asked.

Eli's reflection revealed a heavy sadness. "No, a much wiser author."

We drove on in the quiet darkness, memories of unforgiven sins dancing in the looking glass of the windshield.

Paying a Debt

The sky was just beginning to lighten. Last night's storms were a cooler, purple-clouded memory on the eastern horizon. Lacey fringes of pink lit up their edges. Deeper purple clouds with neon pink edges floated overhead as we arrived at the bus station. It was actually a truck stop, a long squat building with a twenty-four-hour restaurant on one end and a convenience store on the other. A bus line ticket counter was located in the convenience store.

Sitting with Eli in the parking lot, I pulled out the three envelopes. The top one was addressed to Deputy Jeb Barksdale with the sheriff's office address. I held it up so that Eli could see the name. "Guess I don't need this one. I took care of the explanation in person." I tore up the envelope with the letter intended for Jeb inside.

I handed the other two envelopes to Eli, both addressed to the Criminal Investigation Division, Virginia State Police. "Give one of these to Molly. Tell her the story and what to do with this letter if Jeb comes near you or her. Eli, tell her how sorry I am, but I can't stay."

The old man nodded.

"You and Molly watch out for each other."

Eli smiled faintly. "You know that Molly's going to be devastated once she finds out you're gone."

I shook my head. "I doubt that. If she doesn't already know about my past, she will soon. I'm sure she'll be glad to see me out of her life."

Eli smirked, "You're wrong, Joe. You're going to break her heart."

I sighed heavily. "Well, that's not what I want. But whether I'm wrong or right, I'd rather break her heart than put her in danger. I'm a lightning rod and everything near me is scorched by the lightning's strike."

Eli looked off in the distance, somewhere far beyond the parking lot, somewhere far into the past. "I understand, Joe, but I can tell you all too well about the specters that torment you when you break someone's heart. It's a weighty regret that you are shackled with the rest of your life." His eyes grew moist as, unseen, the painful memories danced and chanted again before him. Eli blinked back the tears, turned, and gave me a weak smile.

He extended his hand. "Joe, I've only known you for a few days, but you're already one of my favorite people. You need to come back someday and finish the house."

I shook his hand and smiled. "I'm sure that you'll find the right person to finish what I started." I reached into my pocket and pulled out the small roll of bills remaining from my few days of work. I would need most of it for the bus ticket, but I laid forty-five dollars on the seat between us. From my bag, I retrieved a folded piece of paper. Laying it on top of the money, I slid it toward Eli.

With an inquisitive look on his face, he asked, "What's this?"

I smiled, "Maybe someday I'll stop by for a visit."

Opening the folded paper, he nodded.

"Will you pick up my watch from Willard's?"

He carefully folded the pawn paperwork and tucked it in his shirt pocket. Sliding the forty-five dollars back toward me, he replied, "You keep the money, Joe. You're going to need it." I just stared at the bills and shook my head. He picked up the money and, placing it in my hand, continued, "Keep this. I still owe you."

"I'm pretty sure you've paid me for every hour," I protested.

He chuckled. "Not for the painting. I owe you for helping a cynical old man find hope."

"I'm sorry. I'm lost."

"You and I are from different backgrounds, but we're not so dissimilar." His signature wry smile crept across his face. "We're both haunted by our past. But you're not the same lost soul that wandered into Duke's a few days ago. I can feel it." His smile broadened. "There's hope for you, Joe. And if there's hope for you, then there's hope for a foolish old man who screwed up his life so many years ago. You've shown me that." He paused. "That's a debt that I probably will never be able to repay." He squeezed my fist tightly around the bills. "You keep the money." He patted the papers in his pocket. "The watch is on me. It'll be waiting for you when you come back."

Eli smiled and sighed, "Well, you've got a bus to catch." He took in a deep breath, "And I've got a granddaughter to meet."

I flashed him a big smile.

As I slid out of the passenger seat, Eli called after me, "Take care of yourself, John Smith." I grinned back and waved as I crossed the parking lot.

Things Go South

Walking in, I passed a guy who looked a lot like someone I had seen in the mirror countless times. He was leaning against an old, weathered mailbox. Its faded blue and red paint, only a shadow of brighter days. His clothes were wrinkled and threadbare. His hair was unkempt, and his beard was wild. As I neared, he called out, "Hey man, can you help me out?"

Most people, feeling anxious from the uncertainty of his intentions or maybe from the guilt of their own comfortable circumstances, would brush him off as they hurried on to the important menial tasks of their day. But I stopped to listen.

"I'm trying to get back to my family in Charlotte, but I don't have enough for the bus fare. Can you spare a couple bucks to help?"

I didn't have much money, but I'd been where he was. I dug into my pocket and pulled out a five. "Here you go, buddy. I hope this helps."

He took the five and grinned, "Thanks, thanks so much. I appreciate it."

I pushed through the glass doors into the convenience store. It was a bright, hyperactive collection of candy, food, drinks, novelty, and tourist items. The narrow aisles were lined with shelves packed with brightly colored packages. The walls were plastered with posters, pictures, and screen-printed t-shirts declaring, *Virginia is for Lovers*. A sign over the counter indicated that the bus ticket counter opened at 6:45 a.m. I would have to wait to buy my ticket. Once the counter opened, I would buy a ticket for the first bus headed anywhere and go as far as I could afford.

To kill the time, I walked into the restaurant that made up the other half of the building. It was a dark contrast to the convenience store. Blank white walls, beige polished concrete floors, black metal tables with beige Formica tops, and black metal chairs all arranged in neat, cold rows. This was a soulless place. Not a place where people came to live life. Just a place to eat to stay alive.

Except for a waitress and the kitchen staff, the restaurant was empty. I settled in at a table as far from the entrance as I could. To be safe, I sat facing the door. I wasn't sure that polo shirt had been working alone, and I didn't want another unpleasant surprise. Nervously, I placed my hand in the messenger bag feeling for the gun I'd picked up just hours earlier. The cold metal against my fingers gave me a sense of comfort. I laid the bag in the seat next to me.

I tried to comfort myself with the fact that I now knew that "they" were after me. "They" – the nameless, faceless shadows could be any person in a crowd, in a passing car, or on the street. In the past, I'd been saved by dumb luck. Now, I'd be more careful, but how do you escape a faceless, relentless stalker? I would watch for the suspicious stranger, the unusual circumstance, the unexpected event. My guard was up.

Country music played from speakers in the drop ceiling of the restaurant. I ordered coffee and nursed it to pass the time, listening to the music. It was an old familiar song. What was the name? I struggled to grasp it, but as the refrain played on, it came around, *Just Won't Let Go*. That was it. Sadly, I thought how appropriate the lyrics were. I was having trouble letting go. The refrain played on again.

Seems that I could run forever,
Searching everywhere but never
Find the shelter that I once felt in her soul.
My mind says I should let her
Vanish in the rearview mirror,
But my heart just won't let go.

I'd found a type of peace with Molly. It was hard to explain, but she made me feel important. It was a brief moment that I didn't want to lose. But I was running again, running from my past and now running to stay alive. Eli was right. The measure of success isn't what you gain. It's what you pay to get it. I was paying a terrible price just to stay alive. The song ended and some upbeat country pop tune came on. I lost interest.

At 6:45, I wandered back into the convenience store to see what ride I could arrange. A ticket to Raleigh was the best that I could do, still leaving me some money to eat. I would probably be sleeping under the stars for a while. I bought the ticket and wandered back into the restaurant to wait. I had a couple of hours before departure, so I ordered up my second cup of coffee... followed by a third.

A large man wearing a dark plaid shirt, jeans, and work boots strode into the restaurant. He had long dark hair and a heavy beard. As he scanned the empty room, his eyes fixed on me for a moment, and then he sat facing me at a table near the door. He slid a menu from its resting place between the napkin dispenser and the syrup bottles. I tried to appear uninterested but noticed that he only ordered coffee.

My third cup of coffee now empty, I went looking for the restroom. Washing up, I stared in the mirror. I looked bad. My hair was way too long and needed attention. It had been several days since my last shave. But the most alarming feature was the weary, aging face staring back at me. Stress and the lack of sleep were taking their toll. I'm not sure that people who knew me just two years earlier would recognize me now. As I stared at my reflection, I thought how Molly had been right. My reflection was exactly what I made it. I saw a broken man. I couldn't forgive myself for the monstrous things that I'd been part of. When I looked in the mirror, I only saw my nightmares. I asked out loud to no one but my reflection, "Why am I even running? Why not just let them end it for me?" The reflection staring back from the mirror had no good answer.

I stepped out of the restroom, turning into the restaurant. Anxiously, I searched for plaid shirt. Where was he? I couldn't find him. I was startled by a voice behind me. "Going somewhere, Joe?"

I spun around.

It was Molly.

I was so shaken by the surprise that I scanned the room, still searching for plaid shirt, as I asked, "What are you doing here?"

"Eli told me where to find you. He told me everything–Fayetteville, your arrest, the mysterious deaths of the men in your unit, and last night's horrible events. I know that you can't stay, but I want to go with you."

I shook my head, my eyes darting around the room, my voice low. "Two women are already dead because of me. I can't let you do it."

Her eyes glistened. "You don't get it, do you?" She swept at an escaping tear. "You think you're just damaged goods. You're not."

I still didn't see plaid shirt. "It's not safe. You need to go."

"Go where, Joe? Back to Duke's? Back to Jeb? No."

Tears now streamed down her face. She wiped at them with little success.

"Please, Joe... I've got a car. Everything I own is in the trunk." She attempted a faint smile, but the tears wouldn't stop.

Just then, the panhandler from outside appeared, oblivious to her distress and obviously unaware that I had already contributed to the cause. I understood. He was sleepwalking through a nightmare of a life where people were just shadows against a backdrop of hopelessness. I knew it well.

"Hey, man, can you spare a few bucks? I'm trying to get back to my family in Charlotte."

I looked from the panhandler to Molly. Tears and makeup ran down her face in small streams. I could now see what she had desperately attempted to cover up. There was a bluish-black mark on her left cheek just below her eye.

Suddenly, movement just beyond the window caught my attention. In the parking lot, plaid shirt climbed into the driver's seat of a parked semi and then pulled off. I took a deep breath and exhaled slowly. Shaking my head, I pulled my hand from my pocket and slipped the panhandler my bus ticket. "Here you go. This'll get you as far as Raleigh."

Surprised, the panhandler looked at the ticket and then up at me. He took the ticket thanking me over and over.

Molly looked shocked, seemingly afraid to believe, afraid to be hopeful.

"Come on," I said. "Let's get out of here."

A smile swept across her face as she wiped the tears, smearing the makeup below her eyes and revealing the bruise that wasn't there two days ago. We stepped out into the sunlight of the parking lot.

I felt like a drowning man, breaking the water's surface, gasping in sweet air.

After a few steps, I noticed that Molly wasn't beside me. She'd stopped by the mailbox. She removed something from her jeans pocket and unfolded it. It was the envelope I'd left for Eli to give her.

"I guess I don't need this anymore," she said. Turning, she dropped the envelope into the mailbox. Then, she spun back toward me, beaming.

As she made her way across the parking lot, I closed my eyes for a second. There in a dark corner of my mind, I imagined Si's lifeless body lying on the ground. A rabid pit bull's terror now ended. I opened my eyes and smiled as I took Molly's hand.

In the car, she slid the key in the ignition and then turned to me. Her tear-stained face was still beautiful. She looked at me for a moment, gave a shy smile, and shrugged. She asked, "Where are we going?"

I thought for a moment. "Do you remember telling me about your childhood dream of floating downstream to beautiful golden beaches and deep blue water?"

Molly looked at me with wide, sad eyes, and said, "Those dreams died years ago."

"Nightmares deserve to die, but a dream like that?" I glanced over with a smile. "Well, it deserves to be reborn."

Molly's eyes narrowed.

"Have you ever been to Florida?"

She shook her head. "I've never been out of Virginia."

"Well then, Molly Grover, head south on the interstate. At the tip of Florida, Highway 1 winds its way through miles of islands strung together like a strand of glistening pearls. Bridges carry you over the clearest, blue water you've ever seen. You're going to have your golden sandy beaches and miles and miles of crystal clear, blue water."

She flashed me a smile that was a mix of joy and tearfulness. She lightly touched my hand. Without words, it was the most heartfelt *thank you* I had ever received. At that moment, I felt like the old Joe. Not the one who was broken and haunted but the one who loved and who loved life. There was something warm and healing in her smile, her voice, and her tender touch. I only hoped that I could give her half as much as she gave me.

As we accelerated along the on-ramp, I felt something round in my pocket. I fished it out and smiled. Running my thumb along the surface, I traced the grooved lettering like a blind man soaking in braille text. I closed my eyes, stroking the surface and thinking, *It's the simple gifts that have the deepest meaning.* Looking for a metal surface, I slapped it on the dashboard.

Puzzled, Molly asked, "What's that?"

ELMER SEWARD

Straightening Willard's promotional plastic, digital clock emblazoned with, *Everything You Need*, I said, "It's our new life."

Postscript

The sun poured down like warm butter as we glided along the hallowed path of such great American writers as Ernest Hemingway and Jimmy Buffett. Duvall Street in Key West was alive with the bustle of tourists. Some were lounging in small outdoor garden restaurants with the aroma of Cuban cuisine and conch fritters spilling out into the street. Others searched in small shops for the perfect souvenir to give to relatives and friends or to treasure as keepsakes of a fond vacation. There were those who sought Margaritaville in the small bars serving up frozen beverages and Caribbean-tinged music pulsing to the rhythm of steel drums.

Mopeds, bikes, cars, and pedestrians all ebbed and flowed along the narrow tree-dotted street. Molly clung to my hand as we were swept along with the foot traffic. With wide eyes, she gazed up at the clapboard signs and railed balconies that ran just above us. She squeezed my hand and grinned like a child with a new toy at Christmas. It was all so exciting. Suddenly, she dragged me through the doorway of a small shop. Rows of T-shirts hung from the ceiling and colorful beach towels plastered the walls. The small tight aisles were crammed with seashells and beach-themed trinkets.

As Molly ran her hand along the shelved items, mesmerized by the overwhelming collection of touristabilia, I was drawn to a simple display located near the cash register. There stood two metal, revolving postcard display stands. On one, there were the glossy, slick, professionally photographed cards. Pictures of golden sand and the deep blue ocean; the red, black, and yellow marker at the southernmost point in the United States; Hemingway's House Museum; and the Sunset Festival at Mallory Square were displayed prominently. The other rack displayed reprints of vintage Key West postcards. I slowly turned the second rack, inspecting the old black and white photographs and the painted bridge and sea scenes. But one card grabbed me and wouldn't let go. It wasn't as beautiful as the glossy cards. It was an old color photo of a green road sign that once stood where cars exited Key West. Printed on the sign was the message,

> YOU ARE LEAVING
> KEY WEST, FLA.
> THE BEGINNING OF
> US HIGHWAY 1
> AND ENDING IN
> FORT KENT, ME.

I paid for the card, grabbed a pen, and jotted the address and a quick message.

We've traveled to the southernmost point in the U.S. Some would say we've come to the end of the road, but as the sign says, it's just the beginning. It all depends on the direction you choose. I hope you're at the beginning too.

Then I signed it simply–John Smith.

Just as I finished, Molly slid up next to me, wrapped her arm around my waist, reading over my shoulder. She smiled.

As we moved with the crowd down Duvall Street, we passed a mailbox. I slid the card into the slot, sending it on to a destination I knew only briefly and yet knew so very well.

I closed my eyes for a moment and envisioned Eli shuffling to the mailbox, finding the card, and reading it. With a broad smile, he turns and hands it to a young woman, who, although older, still has a mischievous twinkle in her eyes. While she reads, a little girl in pigtails and a ruffled sundress runs up and tugs on Eli's hand, squealing, "Grandpa, grandpa, come play." All bouncing ruffles and legs, she runs off into the backyard, calling over her shoulder, "Come on, Grandpa. You don't have anything better to do. Do you?" He smiles at a brief recollection and turns to follow.

Looking up at his son-in-law on the ladder, paint spattered and drenched in perspiration, Eli says, "You do mighty fine work. Yes sir, mighty fine." As he nods his head in approval, he adds, "You'd make John Smith proud."

*. *. * *. *

Thanks for reading *Dreams of the Sleepless*.
If you enjoyed the story, please take a second
to rate it. Help others find their next great
read before moving on to your own new
adventure.

Happy Reading,
Elmer

Acknowledgments

I would like to thank my beautiful wife, Mitzi, for all that she has done to make this novel possible. She has been my cheerleader, encouraging me during my frequent spells of self-doubt. On numerous occasions, she has been my sounding board, giving me insight into plot and characters. Her patience with my hours away as I wrote and rewrote this novel has been remarkable. However, her greatest contribution has been as the inspiration for the tenderhearted but determined female characters in my novels. If I have been successful at all in the area of characterization, it is because of her.

I would also like to thank Heather Hernandez for providing valuable feedback and encouragement during revision of this novel. Also, thanks to Scott Cloud for one of his favorite expressions, loosely paraphrased in the book.

Other Books by Elmer Seward

Hearts in the Storm
Set You Free
After the Wanting

Connect with Elmer
website – www.elmerseward.com
Facebook - https://www.facebook.com/ElmerSewardAuthor/
Twitter - @elmerseward2

READ ON FOR A PREVIEW OF
Hearts in the Storm

Excerpt from Hearts in the Storm

Chapter 1

He dragged himself out of the seaside door onto the long, wooden deck. Standing for a moment, he watched the waves whipping up foam as they battered the beleaguered sand. The surging water spewed shells and rocks along the shoreline only to snatch them up, like secrets dredged from the deep, in its frantic retreat. The sea was in constant motion. There was an offshore storm, and the beach was catching the brunt of its fury.

He took a long, slow sip of coffee, hoping to clear the cluttered remnants of last night's bender. Wearing only a tattered pair of shorts, he peered out beneath hooded brows toward the gray and ominous horizon. Even this thickly filtered daylight hurt, as he studied the churning sea.

Laying his cup on the railing, he leaned forward, straining to glimpse the pelicans riding the rolling waves just beyond the break. They'd appear as they crested the top of the swells and then disappear as they slid down into the troughs. Occasionally, one would take flight, circle briefly, and then dive, disappearing beneath the water for a moment.

As he watched, something caught his attention. Just beyond the birds, another dark object in the water appeared and disappeared in the rolling waves. At first, he thought it might be one of the sea birds, but there was something unusual about the shape. Maybe it was a fin. It was common to see dolphins just offshore. It could be a shark fin. They prowled the shoreline more often than the local tourist companies wanted to announce. It crested into view again. No, it was too far out and in the sunless water, too dark to identify but not a fin. It disappeared again. He watched closely, waiting for it to crest. There it was, but it was taller. It was moving. It was an arm. A head and waving arm tossed and swallowed up in the tumultuous water.

The thundering sound of the waves was all-consuming, but faintly, he heard another sound, almost imperceptible. It was a voice in the intermittent roar and crash, a voice crying for help.

He glanced up and down the beach. There was no one else to help. He had to act quickly. Grabbing an old cork safety ring that hung as a decorative prop on the deck, he leaped down the steps to the beach. As he ran, his feet sank into the loose, shifting sand. It felt like he was lifting leaden legs as he struggled forward. Finally reaching the firmer, wet sand, he sped up only to hit the water. Again, each step was like dragging an anvil. He pressed forward into the waves, diving into each one to avoid being knocked backward. As he wrestled in the rush and the roar, he searched desperately to find the person who'd rise and then vanish in the rolling action of the ocean.

Swimming now, fighting against the current determined to rush him back to shore, he was becoming exhausted. The water battered and pulled at him, but he pressed on, trailing the safety ring in his wake.

He was close now. He could see the figure, a girl, maybe in her teens. She flailed her arms, desperately fighting to keep her head above water. She was losing the battle. Alternately, she choked, gasped, and screamed as her head broke the water… only to be sucked down again.

As he swam within feet of the struggling figure, the girl disappeared. He searched the waves that crashed around him. There was no sign of the girl. He dove hoping to find her. The dark, churning water was murky and obscured his vision. Then he saw a hand just below him. He swam deeper, his lungs burning. Now, her face emerged from the darkness. Her eyes were wide with panic as her outstretched fingers clawed desperately. One more stroke propelled him downward. He stretched out to grasp her flailing hands. His fingers were inches away. In the next instant, she was swept away in the shifting current. He peered through the darkness, his lungs about to burst. She was gone.